SUDDENLY, A KNOCK ON THE DOOR

Born in Tel Aviv in 1967, Etgar Keret is one of the leading voices in Israeli literature and cinema. He is the author of five bestselling collections, which have been translated into thirty-one languages. His writing has been published in the *New York Times*, *le Monde*, the *Guardian*, the *New Yorker* and the *Paris Review*. He has also written a number of award-winning screenplays, and *Jellyfish*, his first film as a director along with his wife Shira Geffen, won the Camera d'Or prize for best first feature at Cannes in 2007. In 2010 he was awarded the Chavalier medallion of France's Order of Arts and Letters.

ETGAR KERET

Suddenly, a Knock on the Door

VINTAGE BOOKS
London

Published by Vintage 2013

8 10 9 7

First published in Great Britain in 2012 by
Chatto & Windus

Vintage
Random House, 20 Vauxhall Bridge Road,
London SW1V 2SA

www.vintage-books.co.uk

Addresses for companies within The Random House Group Limited
can be found at: www.randomhouse.co.uk/offices.htm

The Random House Group Limited Reg. No. 954009

A CIP catalogue record for this book
is available from the British Library

ISBN 9780099563327

Penguin Random House is committed to a sustainable future for
our business, our readers and our planet. This book is made from
Forest Stewardship Council® certified paper.

MIX
Paper from
responsible sources
FSC® C018179

Printed and bound in Great Britain by Clays Ltd, St Ives plc

Typeset in Baskerville MT by Palimpsest Book Production Limited,
Falkirk, Stirlingshire

To Shira

CONTENTS

Suddenly, a Knock on the Door

'**Tell** me a story,' the bearded man sitting on my living-room sofa commands. The situation, I must say, is anything but pleasant. I'm someone who writes stories, not someone who tells them. And even that isn't something I do on demand. The last time anyone asked me to tell him a story, it was my son. That was a year ago. I told him something about a fairy and a ferret – I don't even remember what exactly – and within two minutes he was fast asleep. But this situation is fundamentally different. Because my son doesn't have a beard, or a pistol. Because my son asked for the story nicely, and this man is simply trying to rob me of it.

I try to explain to the bearded man that if he puts his pistol away it will only work in his favour, in our favour. It's hard to think up a story with the barrel of a loaded pistol pointed at your head. But the guy insists. 'In this country,' he explains, 'if you want something, you have to use force.' He just got here from Sweden, and in Sweden it's completely different. Over there, if you want something, you ask politely, and most of the time you get it. But not in the stifling, sweaty Middle East. All it takes is one week in this place to figure out how things work – or rather, how things don't work. The Palestinians asked for a state, nicely. Did they get one? Like hell they did. So they switched to blowing up children on buses, and people started listening. The settlers called for a dialogue. Did anyone take them up on it? Of course not. So they started getting physical, pouring hot oil on the border patrolmen, and suddenly they had an audience. In this country, might makes right, and it doesn't matter if it's about politics, or economics or a parking space. Brute force is the only language we understand.

Sweden, the place the bearded man made aliya from, is progressive, and is way up there in quite a few areas. Sweden isn't just Abba or Ikea or the Nobel Prize. Sweden is a world unto itself, and whatever they have, they got by peaceful means. In

Sweden, if he'd gone to the Ace of Base soloist, knocked on her door and asked her to sing for him, she'd invite him in and make him a cup of tea. Then she'd pull out her acoustic guitar from under the bed and play for him. All this with a smile! But here? I mean, if he hadn't been brandishing a pistol I'd have thrown him out right away. 'Look,' I try to reason. '"Look" yourself,' the bearded man grumbles, and cocks his pistol. 'It's either a story or a bullet between the eyes.' I see my choices are limited. The man means business. 'Two people are sitting in a room,' I begin. 'Suddenly there's a knock on the door.' The bearded man stiffens, and for a moment I think maybe the story's getting to him, but it isn't. He's listening to something else. There's a knock on the door. 'Open it,' he tells me, 'and don't try anything. Get rid of whoever it is, and do it fast, or this is going to end badly.'

The young man at the door is doing a survey. He has a few questions. Short ones. About the high humidity here in summer, and how it affects my disposition. I tell him I'm not interested but he pushes his way inside anyway.

'Who's that?' he asks me, pointing at the bearded man standing in my living room. 'That's my nephew from Sweden,' I lie. 'His father died in an avalanche and he's here for the funeral. We're just going over the will. Could you please respect our privacy and leave?' 'C'mon, man,' the pollster says and pats me on the shoulder. 'It's just a few questions. Give a guy a chance to earn a bit of cash. They pay me per respondent.' He flops down on the sofa, clutching his file. The Swede takes a seat next to him. I'm still standing, trying to sound like I mean it. 'I'm asking you to leave,' I tell him. 'Your timing is way off.' 'Way off, eh?' He opens the plastic file and pulls out a big revolver. 'Why's my timing off? Cos I'm darker? Cos I'm not good enough? When it comes to Swedes, you've got all the time in the world. But for a Moroccan, for a war veteran who left pieces of his spleen behind in Lebanon, you can't spare a fucking minute.' I try to reason with him, to tell him it's not that way at all, that he'd simply caught me at a delicate point in my conversation with the Swede. But the pollster raises his revolver to his lips and signals me to shut up. 'Vamos,' he says. 'Stop making excuses. Sit down over there, and out with it.' 'Out with what?' I ask. The truth is, now I'm pretty uptight. The Swede has a pistol too. Things might get out of hand. East is east and west is west, and all that. Different mentalities. Or else the Swede could lose it, simply because he wants the story all to himself. Solo. 'Don't get me started,' the pollster warns. 'I have a short fuse. Out with the story – and make it quick.' 'Yeah,' the Swede chimes in, and pulls out his gun too. I clear my throat, and start all over again. 'Three people are sitting in a room.' 'And no "Suddenly there's a knock on the door",' the Swede announces. The pollster doesn't quite get it, but plays along with him. 'Get on with it,' he says. 'And no knocking on the door. Tell us something else. Surprise us.'

I stop short, and take a deep breath. Both of them are staring at me. How do I always get myself into these situations? I bet things like this never happen to Amos Oz or David Grossman. Suddenly there's a knock on the door. Their gaze turns menacing. I shrug. It's not about me. There's nothing in my story to connect it to that knock. 'Get rid of him,' the pollster orders. 'Get rid of him, whoever it is.' I open the door just a crack. It's a pizza delivery guy. 'Are you Keret?' he asks. 'Yes,' I say, 'but I didn't order a pizza.' 'It says here 14 Zamenhoff Street,' he snaps, pointing at the printed delivery slip and pushing his way inside. 'So what?' I say. 'I didn't order a pizza.' 'Family size,' he insists. 'Half pineapple, half anchovy. Pre-paid. Credit card. Just give me my tip and I'm gone.' 'Are you here for a story too?' the Swede interrogates. 'What story?' the pizza guy asks, but it's obvious he's lying. He's not very good at it. 'Pull it out,' the pollster prods. 'C'mon, out with the pistol right now.' 'I don't have a pistol,' the pizza guy admits awkwardly, and draws a cleaver out from under his cardboard tray. 'But I'll cut him into tiny pieces unless he coughs up a good one, on the double.'

The three of them are on the sofa – the Swede on the right, then the pizza guy, then the pollster. 'I can't do it like this,' I tell them. 'I can't get a story going with the three of you here and your weapons and everything. Go for a walk round the block, and by the time you get back, I'll have something for you.' 'The arsehole's gonna call the police,' the pollster tells the Swede. 'What's he thinking, that we were born yesterday?' 'C'mon, give us one and we'll be on our way,' the pizza guy begs. 'A short one. Don't be so anal. Things are tough, you know. Unemployment, suicide bombings, Iranians. People are hungry for something else. What do you think brought law-abiding guys like us this far? We're desperate, man, desperate.'

I clear my throat and start again. 'Four people are sitting in a room. It's hot. They're bored. The air conditioner's on the blink. One of them asks for a story. The second one joins in, then the third . . .' 'That's not a story,' the pollster protests. 'That's an eyewitness report. It's exactly what's happening here right now. Exactly what we're trying to run away from. Don't you go and dump reality on us like a rubbish truck. Use your imagination, man, create, invent, take it all the way.'

I nod and start again. A man is sitting in a room, all by himself. He's lonely. He's a writer. He wants to write a story. It's been a long time since he wrote his last story, and he misses it. He misses the feeling of creating something out of something. That's right – something out of something. Because something out of nothing is when you make something up out of thin air, in which case it has no value. Anybody can do that. But something out of something means it was really there the whole time, inside you, and you discover it as part of something new, that's never happened before. The man decides to write a story about the situation. Not the political situation and not the social situation either. He decides to write a story about the human situation, the human condition. The human condition the way he's experiencing it right now. But he draws a blank. No story presents itself. Because the human condition the way he's experiencing it right now doesn't seem to be worth a story, and he's just about to give up when suddenly – 'I warned you already,' the Swede interrupts me. 'No knock on the door.' 'I've got to,' I insist. 'Without a knock on the door there's no story.' 'Let him,' the pizza guy says softly. 'Give him a break. You want a knock on the door? OK, have your knock on the door. Just so long as it brings us a story.'

Lieland

Robbie was seven when he told his first lie. His mother had given him a wrinkled old note and asked him to go and buy her a pack of king-size Silk Cuts at the shops. Robbie bought an ice-cream instead. He took the change and hid the coins under a big white stone in the garden of their block of flats, and when his Mother asked him what had happened he told her that a giant, red-headed boy who was missing a front tooth tackled him in the street, slapped him and took the money. She believed him. And Robbie hasn't stopped lying since. When he was in senior school he spent an entire week vegging out on the beach in Eilat, after giving the school counsellor a story about his aunt from Beer Sheba who discovered she had cancer. When he was in the army, this imaginary aunt went blind and saved his arse, big

...t AWOL. No detention, not
...arracks. Nothing. Once, when
...late for work, he'd made up a
...an shepherd he'd found sprawled
out beside ... ...ad. The dog had been run over,
he'd said, and he'd taken it to the vet. In this lie,
the dog was paralysed in two legs, and he'd taken
it to the vet only to find that the dog was never
going to be able to move his hind legs again. That
did the trick. There were lots of lies along the way
in Robbie's life. Lies without arms, lies that were
ill, lies that did harm, lies that could kill. Lies on
foot, or behind the wheel, black-tie lies, and lies
that could steal. He made up these lies in a flash,
never thinking he'd have to cross paths with them
again.

It all started with a dream. A short, fuzzy dream
about his dead mother. In this dream the two of
them were sitting on a straw mat in the middle
of a clear white surface that seemed to have no
beginning and no end. Next to them on this infinite
white surface was a bubble gum machine with a
bubble top, the old-fashioned kind where you put a
coin in the slot, turn the handle – and out comes
a bubble gum. And in his dream, Robbie's mother

told him that the afterworld was driving her up the wall, because the people were good, but there were no cigarettes. Not just no cigarettes, no coffee. No radio. Nothing.

'You have to help me, Robbie,' she said. 'You have to buy me a bubble gum. I raised you, son. All these years I gave you everything and asked for nothing. But now it's time to give something back to your old mum. Buy me a bubble gum. A red one, if you can, but blue is OK too.' And in his dream, Robbie kept rummaging through his pockets, hoping to find some change. Nothing. 'I don't have any, Mum,' he said, the tears welling up in his eyes. 'I don't have any change. I went through all my pockets.'

Considering that he never cried when he was awake, it was strange to be crying in his dream. 'Did you look under the stone?' his mother asked and clasped his hand in her own. 'Maybe the coins are still there?'

And then he woke up. It was 5 a.m. on a Saturday, and still dark outside. Robbie found himself getting into the car and driving to the place where he had lived as a little boy. With no traffic on the road, it took him less than twenty minutes to get there. On the ground floor of the building, where Pliskin's grocer's had once been, there was a pound shop, and next to it, instead of the shoe mender there was a mobile phone shop offering upgrades like there was no tomorrow.

But the building itself hadn't changed. More than twenty years had gone by since they'd moved out, and it hadn't even been repainted. The garden was still the same too, a few flowers, a tap, a rusty water meter, weeds. And in the corner, next to the clothes lines, was the white stone, just lying there.

He stood in the back garden of the building where he'd grown up, wearing his parka, holding a big plastic torch, feeling strange. Five thirty on a Saturday morning. Let's say a neighbour turned up – what would he say? My dead mother appeared in my dream and asked me to buy her a bubble gum, so I came here to look for some change?

Strange that the stone was still there, after all those years. Then again, if you thought about it, it's not as if stones just get up and walk away. He picked it up, gingerly, as if there might be a scorpion hiding beneath it. But there was no scorpion, and no snake either, and no coins. Just a hole the width of a grapefruit, and a light shining out of it.

Robbie tried to peek into the hole, but the light dazzled him. He hesitated for a second, then reached in. Lying on the ground, he extended his arm all the way up to his shoulder, trying to touch something at the bottom. But there was no bottom and the only thing he could reach was made of cold metal and felt like a handle. The handle of a bubble gum machine. Robbie turned it as hard as he could and felt the handle respond to his touch. This was the moment the bubble gum should have rolled out. This was exactly when it should have made its way from the metallic innards of the machine into the hand of the little boy waiting impatiently for it to emerge. This was exactly the moment when all those things were supposed to happen. But they didn't. And as soon as Robbie had finished turning the handle, he'd turned up here.

'Here' was a different place, but a familiar one too. It was the place from his dream. Stark white, no walls, no floor, no ceiling, no sunshine. Just whiteness and a bubble gum machine. A bubble gum machine and a sweaty, ugly, red-headed boy.

Suddenly, a Knock on the Door

Somehow, Robbie hadn't noticed him before, and just as Robbie was about to smile at the boy or to say anything at all, the redhead kicked him in the shins, as hard as he could, and Robbie dropped to the ground, writhing in pain. With Robbie down on his knees, he and the boy were now the same height. The boy looked Robbie in the eye, and even though Robbie knew they'd never met, there was something familiar about him. 'Who are you?' he asked the boy, who was standing in front of him. 'Me?' the boy answered, showing a mean smile with a missing front tooth. 'I'm your first lie.'

Robbie struggled to his feet. His leg hurt like hell. The boy himself was long gone. Robbie studied the bubble gum machine. In between the round bubble gums there were half-transparent plastic balls with trinkets inside them. He rummaged through his pockets for some change, but then remembered that the boy had grabbed his wallet before he ran off.

Robbie limped away, in no particular direction. Since there was nothing to go by on the white surface, except the bubble gum machine, all he could do was try to move away from it. Every few steps, he turned round to make sure the machine was becoming smaller.

At one point, he turned round to discover a German shepherd standing next to a skinny old man with a glass eye and no arms. The dog he recognised at once, by the way it half crawled forward, its two forelegs struggling to pull its paralysed pelvis along. It was the run-over dog from his lie. It was panting with the effort and excitement, and was happy to see him. It licked Robbie's hand and looked at him intently with glistening eyes. Robbie couldn't quite place the skinny old man.

'I'm Robbie,' he said.

'I'm Igor,' the old man introduced himself, and gave Robbie a pat with one of his hooks.

'Do we know each other?' Robbie asked, after a few seconds' awkward silence.

'No,' Igor said, lifting the lead with one of his hooks. 'I'm only here because of him. He sniffed you from miles away and got worked up. He wanted us to come.'

'So, there's no connection – between us?' Robbie asked. He felt a sense of relief as he said this.

'Me and you? No, no connection whatsoever. I'm somebody else's lie.'

Robbie almost asked whose lie he was but he was afraid the question might be considered rude in this place. For that matter, he'd have liked to ask what this place was exactly and whether there were a lot more people there, or more lies, or whatever they called themselves, other than him. But he thought it might be a sensitive topic and that he shouldn't bring it up just yet. So instead of talking, he patted Igor's handicapped dog. It was a nice dog, and it seemed happy to meet Robbie, who wished his lie had a little less pain and suffering in it.

'The bubble gum machine,' he asked Igor, when a few minutes had passed. 'What coins does it take?'

'Liras,' the old man said.

Robbie said, 'There was a boy here just now. He took my wallet. But even if he hadn't, there wouldn't be any liras in it.'

'A boy with a tooth missing?' Igor asked. 'That little scum bag steals from everyone. He even eats the dog's dried food. Where I come from, in Russia, they'd take a boy like that and stick him out in the snow in nothing but his underwear, and they wouldn't let him back in the house until his whole body turned blue.' With one of his hooks, Igor pointed to his back pocket. 'In there I've got some liras. Help yourself. It's on me.'

Robbie hesitated, but he took a lira coin out of Igor's pocket, and after thanking him, offered to give him his Swatch in return.

'Thanks,' Igor nodded. 'But what would I do with a plastic watch? Besides, I'm in no hurry to get anywhere.'

When he saw Robbie looking around for something else to give him, Igor stopped him and said, 'I owe you anyway. If you hadn't made up that lie about the dog, I'd be all alone. So now we're even.'

Robbie hobbled back as quickly as he could in the direction of the bubble gum machine. He was still smarting from the redhead's kick, but less so now. He dropped the lira into the slot, took a deep breath, closed his eyes and turned the handle.

He found himself stretched out on the ground in the garden of their old building. The dawn light was painting the sky dark shades of blue. Robbie pulled his arm out of the hole in the ground. And when he opened his fist, there was a red bubble gum inside.

Before he left, he put the stone back in its place. He didn't ask himself about the hole and what exactly had happened down there. He just got in the car, reversed and drove away. The red bubble gum he put under his pillow, for his mother, in case she came back in his dream.

At first, Robbie thought about it a lot, about that place, about the dog, about Igor, about other lies he'd told – lies he was lucky enough not to have to meet again. There was that bizarre lie he'd told his ex-girlfriend, Ruthie, when he couldn't make it to Friday-night dinner at her parents' house – about this niece of his who lived in Natanyah whose husband beat her up, and about how the guy had threatened to kill her, so Robbie had to go over there to help calm things down. To this day, he had no idea why he'd made up such a twisted story. Maybe at the time he thought that the more complicated and warped it was, the more likely Ruthie was to believe him. Some people, when they bail out of Friday-night dinner, say they've got a headache or something. Not him.

Instead, because of him and those stories of his, a lunatic husband and a battered wife were out there, not far away, in a hole in the ground.

He didn't go back to the hole, but something about that place stayed with him. At first, he continued to tell lies, but they were the kind where nobody hits anybody and nobody limps or dies of cancer. For example: he was late for work because he had to water the plants in his aunt's flat while she was visiting her successful son in Japan. Or: he was late for a baby shower because a cat just had kittens on his doorstep and he had to take care of the litter. Stuff like that.

But it was much harder to make up all the positive lies. At least if you wanted them to sound plausible. In general if you tell people something bad, they don't question it, because it strikes them as normal. But when you make up good things, they get suspicious. And so, very gradually, Robbie found himself winding down the lies. Out of laziness, mostly. And with time, he thought less and less about that place. About the hole. Until the morning when he overheard Natasha from Accounting talking to her boss. Her uncle Igor had had a heart attack and she needed some time off. Poor man – a widower, who'd already lost both arms in an accident in Russia. And now, his heart. He was so alone, so helpless.

The head of Accounting granted her time off right away, no questions asked. She went to her office, took her bag and left the building. Robbie followed Natasha to her car. When she stopped to get her keys out of her bag, he stopped too. She turned round. 'You work in Acquisitions, don't you?' she asked. 'Aren't you Zaguri's assistant?'

'Yeah,' Robbie said, nodding. 'My name's Robbie.'

'Hi, Robbie,' Natasha said with a nervous Russian smile. 'So what's up? You need something?'

'It's about that lie you told, earlier, to the head of Accounting,' Robbie stammered. 'I know him.'

'You followed me all the way to my car just to accuse me of being a liar?'

'No,' said Robbie. 'I didn't mean to accuse you. Really. Your being a liar is fine. I'm a liar too. But this Igor from your lie, I met him. He's one in a million. And you – if you don't mind my saying so – you've made things pretty hard for him as it is. So I just wanted to—'

'Would you get out of my way?' Natasha

interrupted him icily. 'You're blocking the door of my car.'

'I know this sounds far-fetched, but I can prove it,' Robbie said, feeling more and more uneasy. 'This Igor doesn't have an eye. I mean, he does, but only one. At one point, you must have made up something about how he'd lost an eye, yes?'

Natasha was already getting into her car, but she stopped. 'Where d'you get that from? Are you a friend of Slava's?'

'I don't know any Slava,' Robbie muttered. 'Just Igor. Really. If you want, I can take you to him.'

They were standing in the back garden of his old building. Robbie moved the stone aside, lay down on the damp soil and pushed his arm all the way into the hole. Natasha was standing over him. He held out his other arm and said: 'Hold on tight.'

Natasha looked at the man stretched out at her feet. Thirty-something, good-looking, in a clean, ironed, white shirt, which was already slightly less clean and much less ironed. His one arm was stuck in the hole, his cheek was glued to the ground.

'Hold tight,' he said. And as she held out her hand to him, she couldn't help wondering how it was she always ended up with the nutters. When he'd started with that crap by the car, she thought maybe it was a sweet way of chatting her up, but now she realised that this man with the soft eyes and the bashful smile really was a nutcase. His fingers were clasping hers. They stayed that way, frozen, for a minute or so, him on the ground, and her standing over him, slightly stooped, looking bewildered.

'OK,' Natasha whispered in a gentle, almost therapeutic voice. 'So we're holding hands. Now what?'

'Now,' Robbie said, 'I'll turn the handle.'

It took them a long time to find Igor. First they met a hairy, hunchbacked lie, evidently Argentinian, who spoke nothing but Spanish. Then, another of Natasha's lies – an overzealous policeman with a yarmulke, who insisted on detaining them and checking their papers, but he'd never even heard of Igor. In the end the person who helped them was Robbie's battered niece from Natanyah. They found her feeding the kittens from his most recent lie. She hadn't seen Igor for a few days, but she knew where to find his dog. As for the dog, once it finished licking Robbie's hands and face, it was glad to take them to Igor's bedside.

Igor was in a pretty bad way. His complexion was sallow and he was sweating heavily. But when he saw Natasha, his face lit up. He was so thrilled that he hauled himself up and hugged her, even though he could hardly stand. At that point, Natasha began to cry and asked him to forgive her because this Igor wasn't just one of her lies, he was also her uncle. A made-up uncle, but still. And Igor told her she shouldn't feel bad, the life she invented for him may not always have been easy, but he'd enjoyed every minute of it, and she had nothing to worry about, because compared to the train crash in Minsk, the stick-up in Odessa, the lightning that struck him in Vladivostok and the pack of rabid wolves in Siberia, this heart attack was nothing. And when they got back to the bubble gum machine, Robbie put in a one-lira coin, took Natasha's hand and asked her to turn the handle.

Once they were back in the garden, Natasha found herself holding a plastic ball, with a trinket inside: an ugly, gold-coloured charm in the shape of a heart.

'You know,' she said, 'I was supposed to be going to Sinai tonight with a friend, for a few days, but I think I'm going to call it off, and go back tomorrow to take care of Igor. Would you like to come too?'

Robbie nodded. He knew that if he wanted to join her, he'd have to come up with another lie at the office. He wasn't quite sure what it would be. All he knew was that it would be a happy lie, full of light, flowers and sunshine. And who knows – maybe even a baby or two, and they'd be smiling.

Cheesus Christ

Have you ever wondered which word is most frequently uttered by people about to die a violent death? MIT carried out a comprehensive study of the question among heterogeneous communities in North America and discovered that the word is none other than 'fuck'. Eight per cent of those about to die say 'what the fuck', 6 per cent say only 'fuck', and there's another 2.8 per cent that say 'fuck you', though in their case, of course, 'you' is the last word, even if 'fuck' over-shadows it irrefutably. And what does Jeremy Kleinman say a minute before he checks out? He says, 'Without cheese.' Jeremy says that because he's ordering something in a cheeseburger restau-rant called Cheesus Christ. They don't have plain hamburgers on the menu, so Jeremy, who keeps kosher, asks for a cheeseburger without cheese.

The shift manager in the restaurant doesn't make a big deal out of it. Lots of customers have asked her for that in the past, so many that she felt the need to report on it in a series of detailed emails to the CEO of the Cheesus Christ chain whose office is in Atlanta. She suggested that he add a plain hamburger to the menu. 'A lot of people ask me for it, but at the moment, they have to order a cheeseburger without cheese, which is cagey and a little embarrassing. It's embarrassing for me, and, if you don't mind my saying so, for the whole chain. It makes me feel like a technocrat, and for the customers, the chain comes across as an inflexible organisation they have to trick in order to get what they want.' The CEO never replied to her emails, and for her, that was even more embarrassing and humiliating than all those times customers asked her for cheeseburgers without cheese. When a dedicated employee turns to her employer with a problem, especially one related to the workplace, the least he could do is acknowledge her existence. The CEO could have written to say that it was being handled or that, while he appreciated her turning to him, he unfortunately couldn't make any changes to the menu, or a million other bullshit replies of that kind. But he didn't. He didn't write anything. And that made her feel like she was invisible. Just like that night in New Haven when her boyfriend Nick started chatting up the waitress while she herself was sitting next to him at the bar. She'd cried then, and Nick hadn't even known why, and that same night, she'd packed her things and left. Mutual friends had called a few weeks later to tell her Nick had killed himself. None of them openly blamed her for what happened, but there was something in the way they told her about it, something accusing, though she couldn't even say what. Anyway when the CEO didn't answer her emails, she thought about quitting her job. But what happened with Nick stopped her from doing that, and it wasn't as if she thought the CEO of Cheesus Christ would commit suicide when he heard that the shift manager of some crappy branch in the north-east had quit, but still. The truth is that if the CEO had heard she'd quit because of him, he actually would have killed himself. The truth is that if the CEO had heard that the African white lion had become extinct because of illegal hunting, he would have killed himself. He would even have killed himself after hearing something more trivial – for instance, that it was going to rain tomorrow. The CEO of the Cheesus Christ restaurant chain suffered from severe clinical depression. His colleagues at work knew that, but were careful not to spread this painful fact around, mostly because they respected his privacy, but also because it could have instantly sent stock prices crashing. After all, what does the stock market sell us if not the unfounded hope of a rosy future? And a CEO with clinical depression is not exactly the ideal ambassador for that kind of message. The CEO of Cheesus Christ, who totally understood how problematic his emotional state was, both personally and publicly, tried medication. That didn't help at all. The pills were prescribed to him by a doctor from Iraq who had been granted refugee status in the US after his family was accidentally blown up by an F-16 trying to assassinate Saddam Hussein's sons. His wife, father and two small sons were killed, and only his older daughter, Suha, survived. In an interview on CNN, the doctor said that despite his personal tragedy, he wasn't angry with the American people. But the truth is that he was. He was more than angry. He was boiling with rage at the American people. But he knew that if he wanted a green card, he had to lie about it. As he lied, he thought about his dead family and his living daughter. He lied because he believed that an American education would be good for her. How wrong he was. His daughter became pregnant at fifteen by some fat white trash kid who was a year ahead of her at school and refused to acknowledge the baby. Due to complications at birth, the baby was born retarded. In the States, just like almost anywhere else, when you're a fifteen-year-old single mother of a retarded child, for all intents and purposes, your fate is sealed. There's probably some made-for-TV movie that claims that isn't the case, that you can still find love and have a career and who knows what else. But that's only a movie. In real life, the minute they told her that her baby was retarded it was as if a 'game over' sign in neon lights was flashing in the air above her head. Maybe if her father had told the truth on CNN and they hadn't come to the States, her fate would have been different. And if Nick hadn't hit on that bottle blonde in the bar, his situation and the shift manager's would have been much better too. And if the CEO of the Cheesus Christ chain had got the right medication, his situation would have been just great. And if that crazy guy in the cheeseburger restaurant hadn't stabbed Jeremy Kleinman, Jeremy Kleinman's state would be alive, which, in most people's opinion, is a lot better than the dead state he now found himself in. He didn't die straight away. He gasped, tried to say something, but the shift manager, who was holding his hand, told him not to speak, to save his strength. He didn't speak, he tried to save his strength. Tried, but couldn't. There's a theory, also out of MIT I think, about the butterfly effect: a butterfly flutters its wings on a beach in Brazil, and as a result, a tornado starts up on the other side of the world. The tornado appears in the original example. They could have thought up a different example in which the flutter of butterfly wings causes badly needed rain, but the scientists who developed the theory chose a tornado, and not because, like the CEO of Cheesus Christ, they were clinically depressed. It's because the scientists who specialise in probability know that the chance of something detrimental occurring is a thousand times greater than the chance of something beneficial happening.

'Hold my hand,' is what Jeremy Kleinman wanted to say to the shift manager as his life leaked out of him like chocolate milk from a punctured carton. 'Hold it and don't let go, whatever happens.' But he didn't say that because she asked him not to speak. He didn't say that because he didn't need to – she held his sweaty hand till he died. For a long time after that, actually. She held his hand till the paramedics asked her if she was his wife. Three days later, she got an email from the CEO. That incident in her branch had made him decide to sell the chain and retire. The decision brought him far enough out of his depression to make him start answering his emails. He answered them from his laptop, sitting on a gorgeous beach in Brazil. In his long email, he wrote that she was absolutely right and he would pass on her carefully reasoned request to the new CEO. As he pressed 'send', his finger touched the wings of a butterfly sleeping on the keyboard. The butterfly fluttered its wings. Somewhere on the other side of the world, evil winds began to blow.

Simyon

Two people were standing at the door. A second lieutenant wearing a knitted yarmulke, and behind him, a thin officer with sparse, light-coloured hair and captain's bars on her shoulders. Orit waited a minute, and when she saw that they weren't saying anything, she asked if she could help them. 'Druckman,' the captain tossed the word, part command, part reprimand, at the soldier. 'It's about your husband,' the religious soldier mumbled at Orit. 'Can we come in?' Orit smiled and said that this must be some kind of mistake because she wasn't married. The captain looked down at the wrinkled note she was holding and asked if her name was Orit, and when Orit said yes, the captain said politely but firmly, 'Could we come in for a minute anyway?' Orit led them into the living room of the place she shared with her flatmate. Before she had a chance to offer them something to drink, the religious soldier blurted out, 'He's dead.' 'Who?' Orit asked. 'Why now?' the captain rebuked him. 'Can't you wait a second for her to sit down? To get herself a glass of water?' 'I apologise,' the religious soldier said to Orit, clenching his lips in a nervous twitch. 'This is my first. I'm still training.' 'It's all right,' Orit said, 'But who's dead?' 'Your husband,' the religious soldier said. 'I don't know whether you heard, but this morning there was a terrorist attack at the Beit Leed junction . . .' 'No,' Orit said, 'I haven't heard. I don't listen to the news. But it doesn't matter anyway because this is a mistake. I told you, I'm not married.' The religious soldier gave the captain a pleading look. 'You're Orit Bielsky?' the captain asked in a slightly impatient voice. 'No,' Orit said, 'I'm Orit Levine.' 'Right,' the captain replied. 'Right. And in February two years ago, you married First Sergeant Simyon Bielsky.' Orit sat down on the torn living-room sofa. The inside of her throat was so dry that it itched. On second thoughts, it really would've been better if Druckman had waited till she got herself a glass of Diet Coke before starting. 'So I don't get it,' the religious soldier whispered out loud. 'Is it her or isn't it?' The captain signalled him to shut up. She went over to the kitchen sink and brought back a glass of water for Orit. The water from the tap in the flat was disgusting. Orit always thought water was disgusting, especially the water in this flat. 'Take your time,' the captain said, handing Orit the glass. 'We're in no rush,' she said and sat down beside her. They sat like that, in absolute silence, until the religious soldier, who was still standing, started to lose his patience and said, 'He didn't have any family here, you probably know that?' Orit nodded. 'They all stayed in Russia or the CIS, or whatever they call it now. He was completely alone.' 'Except for you,' the captain said, touching Orit's hand with her own dry one. 'Do you know what that means?' Druckman asked, sitting down on an armchair across from them. 'Shut up,' the captain hissed at him. 'You idiot.' 'Why idiot?' the religious soldier asked, insulted. 'We'll have to tell her in the end anyway, so why drag it out?' The captain ignored him and gave Orit an awkward hug that seemed to embarrass them both. 'Have to tell me what?' Orit asked, trying to extricate herself from the hug. The captain let go, took a slightly theatrical deep breath and said, 'You're the only one who can identify him.'

She'd met Simyon for the first time on the day they got married. He was serving on the same base as Assi, and Assi always used to tell her stories about him, how he wore his trousers so high that every morning he had to decide which side to put his prick on, and how every time they listened to the shout-outs to soldiers on the radio, when the announcer said something like 'To the sexiest soldier in the army', Simyon would always tense up, as if the message was one hundred per cent for him. 'Who could be sending a message to that schmuck?' Assi would say, laughing. And that's the schmuck she married. The truth was that she'd suggested to Assi that he should be the one to marry her so she wouldn't have to serve in the army, but Assi said no way, because a fictitious marriage to a boyfriend was never completely fictitious, and it was a sure way to mess things up. He was also the one who suggested Simyon. 'For a hundred shekels, that moron would even give you a baby,' Assi said with a laugh. 'For a hundred shekels, those Russians would do anything.' She told Assi that she had to think about it, even though in her heart she'd already agreed. But he'd hurt her feelings when he said he wouldn't marry her. She was just asking him for a favour and a boyfriend should know how to help when he's needed. Anyway, even if it was only fictitious, it was no fun being married to a schmuck.

The next day, Assi came home from the base, planted a wet kiss on her forehead and said, 'I saved you a hundred shekels.' Orit wiped the saliva off her forehead and Assi explained: 'That moron will marry you for free.' Orit said that seemed a little suspicious and they had to be careful, because maybe this Simyon didn't really understand what the word 'fictitious' meant. 'Oh, he understands all right,' Assi said and started foraging around in the fridge. 'He may be a complete idiot, but he's cagey like you wouldn't believe.' 'So why did he agree to do it for free?' Orit asked. 'How do I know?' Assi said, laughing and taking a bite of an unwashed cucumber. 'Maybe he thought that it was as close to being married he'd ever get in this life.'

*   *   *

The captain drove the Renault and the religious soldier sat in the back. They were quiet almost all the way, and that left Orit a lot of time to think about the fact that she was going to see a dead person for the first time in her life, and that she always found herself bastards for boyfriends and that even though she knew it from the first minute she still always stayed with them for a year or two. She thought about the abortion and about her mother, who believed in reincarnation and insisted afterwards that the baby's soul was reincarnated in her scrawny cat. 'Listen to the way he's crying,' she told Orit. 'Listen to his voice, it's like a baby's. You've had him for four years and he's never cried like that before.' Orit knew that her mother was talking crap and that the cat was just sniffing food or some female cat through the window. Except that his yowling really did sound a bit like a baby crying and he kept at it all night. Her only piece of luck was that she and Assi weren't together any more, because if she'd told him something like that, he would have burst out laughing. She tried to think about Simyon's soul too and where it had been reincarnated, but she reminded herself that she didn't believe in any of that. Then she asked herself why she'd agreed to go to the morgue with the officers, and why she hadn't mentioned that the marriage was fictitious. There was something weird about going to a morgue and identifying a husband. Scary, but exciting too. It was a little like being in a film – having the experience without paying the price. Assi would probably say that it was a terrific opportunity to get a lifetime widow's pension from the army without even lifting a finger, and no one in the army could do anything against a marriage contract from the rabbinate. 'It'll be fine,' said the captain, who must have noticed the worry lines in Orit's forehead. 'We'll be with you the whole time.'

Assi came to the rabbinate as Simyon's witness, and throughout the ceremony he made faces, trying to get Orit to laugh. Simyon himself looked a lot better than the stories about him made out. Not a world-class hunk, but not as ugly as Assi had described him. And he wasn't such an idiot either. He was very strange, but not stupid, and after the rabbinate, Assi took them out for falafel. That whole day, Simyon and Orit didn't exchange a word except for 'hello' and the words they had to speak at the ceremony, and later at the falafel stand, they tried hard not to look at each other. That made Assi laugh. 'Look at how pretty your wife is,' he said, putting his hand on Simyon's shoulder. Simyon kept his eyes fixed on the dripping pitta bread he was holding. 'What are we going to do with you, Simyon?' Assi said, still needling him. 'You know that now you have to kiss her. Otherwise, according to Jewish law, the marriage isn't valid.' To this day, she doesn't really know whether Simyon believed him. Assi told her later that of course he hadn't, and that he was just taking advantage of the situation, but Orit wasn't so sure. In any case, he suddenly bent forward and tried to kiss her. Orit jumped back, and his lips didn't touch hers. But the smell from his mouth did, blending with the smell of frying falafel oil and that mouldy smell of the rabbinate that clung to her hair. She took a few steps away from them and vomited into a flower bed, and when she looked up, her eyes met Simyon's. He froze for a minute and then started to run, to get away. Assi tried to call him back, but he didn't stop. And that was the last time she saw him. Till today.

On the way to the morgue, she was afraid she

wouldn't be able to identify him. After all, she'd only seen him once, two years ago, and he was alive and well then. But now she knew right away that it was him. A green sheet covered his body up to his neck. His face was completely intact, except for a small hole no larger than a one shekel coin in his cheek. And the smell of the corpse was just like the smell of his breath on her face two years ago. She'd thought about that moment many times. While they were still at the falafel stand, Assi had told her that it wasn't her fault that Simyon had bad breath, but she always felt like it was. And today, when they knocked on the door, she should have remembered him. It wasn't as if she'd got married a million times or anything. 'Do you want us to give you a minute alone with your husband?' the captain asked. Orit shook her head. 'Really. It's OK to cry,' the captain said. 'There's no point in holding it in.'

Shut

I know a man who fantasises all the time. I mean, this man even walks down the street with his eyes shut. One day, I'm sitting in the passenger seat of his car and I look over to the left and see him with both his hands on the wheel and his eyes shut. I'm serious, he was driving like that on a main road.

'Haggai,' I say, 'that's not a good idea. Haggai, open your eyes.' But he keeps driving like everything's fine.

'You know where I am now?' he asks me.

'Open your eyes,' I say again, 'come on, it's freaking me out.' Miraculously, we didn't crash.

The man would fantasise about other people's homes, that they were his. About their cars, about their jobs. Never mind their jobs. About his wife. He'd imagine that other women were his wife. And children too, kids he met in the street or the park, or saw on some TV series, imagining they were his family instead of his own kids. He'd spend hours doing it. If it was up to him, he'd spend his whole life at it.

'Haggai,' I say to him, 'Haggai, wake up. Wake up to your own life. You have an amazing life. A fantastic wife. Great kids. Wake up.'

'Stop,' he answers from the depth of his beanbag, 'don't ruin it. You know who I'm with now? Yotam Ratsabi, my old army buddy. I'm on a jeep tour with Yotam Ratsabi. Just me, Yoti and little Eviatar Mendelssohn. He's this smart-arse kid from Amit's nursery. And Eviatar, the little devil, says to me, "Dad, I'm thirsty. Can I have a beer?" Picture it. The boy's not seven yet. So I say, "No beer, Evi. You know Mum says it's not allowed." His mum, my ex, I mean. Rona Yedidia from school. Beautiful as a model, but tough, tough as nails.'

'Haggai,' I say, 'he's not your son and she's not your wife. You're not divorced, man, you're happily married. Open your eyes.'

'Every time I bring the boy home to her, I get a hard-on,' he says, as if he doesn't hear me. 'A hard-on as big as a ship's mast. She's beautiful, my ex, beautiful but tough. And that toughness is what gives me a hard-on.'

'She's not your ex,' I say, 'and you don't have a hard-on.' I know what I'm talking about. He's a metre away from me in his shorts. No hard-on there.

'We had to split up,' he says, 'I hated being with her. And she hated being with herself too.'

'Haggai,' I plead, 'your wife's name is Carnie. And yes, she's beautiful. But she's not tough. Not with you.' His wife is really soft. She has the gentle soul of a bird and a big heart; she feels for everybody. We've been together for nine months now. Haggai starts work early, so I go to see her at eight thirty, just after she drops the kids off at nursery.

'Rona and I met at school,' he goes on. 'She was my first and I was hers. After the divorce, I fucked around a lot, but none of the women even came close to her. And, you know, at least from a distance, she looks like she's still alone. If I found out she has someone, it would shatter me, even though we're divorced and everything. Shatter me into pieces. I just wouldn't be able to take it. None of the other women mean anything. Just her. She's the one who's always been there.'

'Haggai,' I say, 'her name's Carnie and no one's with her. You're still married.'

'No one's with Rona either,' he says, and licks his dry lips, 'no one. I'd kill myself if there was.'

Carnie comes into the flat now, carrying a shopping bag. She tosses a casual 'hi' in my direction. Since we've been together, she tries to be more distant when other people are around. She doesn't even say hi to Haggai; she knows there's no point talking to him when his eyes are shut.

'My house,' he says, 'right in the centre of Tel Aviv. Beautiful, with a mulberry tree right outside the window. But it's small, way too small. I need another room. On the weekends, when I have the kids, I have to get out the sofa-bed. It's a real pain in the neck. If I don't find a solution by the summer, I'll just have to move.'

Healthy Start

Every night, since she left, he'd fall asleep in a different spot: on the sofa, in an armchair in the living room, on the mat on the balcony like some homeless bum. And every morning, he'd make a point of going out for breakfast. Even prisoners get a daily walk in the yard, don't they? At the cafe they always gave him a table set for two, and sat him opposite an empty chair. Always. Even when the waiter specifically asked him if he was alone. Other people would be sitting there in twos or threes, laughing or tasting each other's food, or fighting over the bill, while Miron sat by himself eating his Healthy Start – orange juice, muesli with honey, decaf double espresso with warm low-fat milk on the side. Of course it would have been nicer if someone were sitting down opposite him and laughing with him, if there had been someone to argue with over the bill, and he'd have to struggle, to hand the money to the waitress saying, 'Don't take it from him! Avri, put it back. This one's on me.' But he didn't really have anyone to do that with, and breakfast alone in a cafe was a hundred times better than staying at home.

Miron spent a lot of time eyeing the other tables. He'd eavesdrop on conversations, read the Sports supplement or examine the ups and downs of the Israeli shares on Wall Street with an air of detached concern. Sometimes someone would come over and ask for a section of the paper he'd finished reading, and he would nod and try to smile. Once, when a sexy young mother with a baby in a pushchair walked over to him he even said to her, as he gave up the front page with the headline about a gang rape in the suburbs: 'What a crazy world we're bringing our children into.' He thought it sounded like the kind of statement that brings people closer together, pointing as it did to their common fate, but the sexy mum just glared at him, and took the Healthy Living supplement too without asking.

Then one Thursday a fat, sweaty man walked into the cafe and smiled at him. Miron was caught off guard. The last person who'd given him a smile was Maayan, just before she left him, five months earlier, and her smile had been unmistakably sarcastic, whereas this one was soft, almost apologetic. The fat man gestured something, apparently a signal that he'd like to sit down, and Miron nodded almost without thinking. The fat man took a seat.

'Reuben,' he said, 'listen, I'm really sorry I'm late. I know we said ten but I had a nightmare morning with the kid.'

It crossed Miron's mind that maybe he ought to tell the fat man he wasn't Reuben, but he found himself checking his watch instead, and saying, 'What's ten minutes? Forget it.'

Then neither of them spoke for a second, and Miron asked if the kid was OK. And the fat man said she was, it was just that she'd started a new nursery, and every time he took her there she didn't want him to leave.

'But never mind,' he stopped short. 'You've got enough on your plate without my problems. Let's get down to business.'

Miron took a deep breath and waited.

'Look,' the fat man said, 'five hundred is too

high. Give it to me for four hundred. Know what? Four hundred and ten, even, and I'm good for six hundred pieces.'

'Four hundred and eighty,' Miron said. 'Four hundred and eighty. And that's only if you're good for a thousand.'

'You've got to understand,' the fat man said, 'the market's in the shit, what with the recession and everything. Just last night on the news they showed people eating out of rubbish bins. If you keep pushing, I'll have to sell high. You're pricing me right out of the market.'

'Don't worry,' Miron told him. 'For every three people eating out of rubbish bins, there's someone driving a Mercedes.'

This made the fat man laugh out loud. 'They told me you were tough,' he muttered with a smile.

'I'm just like you,' Miron protested. 'Simply trying to keep body and soul together.'

The fat man wiped his sweaty palm on his shirt, then held it out. 'Four hundred and sixty,' he said. 'Four hundred and sixty and I take a thousand.' When he saw Miron wasn't reacting, he added: 'Four hundred and sixty, a thousand pieces, and I owe you a favour. And you know better than anyone, Reuben, that in our business favours are worth more than money.'

This last sentence was all Miron needed to take the outstretched hand and shake it. For the first time in his life, someone owed him a favour. Someone who thought his name was Reuben, but still. And when they'd finished eating, as they argued over who would pay, a warm feeling spread through Miron's stomach. He beat the fat man to it by a tenth of a second and shoved the crumpled note into the waitress's hand.

From that day on it became practically standard procedure. Miron would find a table, give his order and keep a lookout for any new person who came into the cafe, and if that person started searching the room with an expectant look, Miron would quickly wave and invite him or her to join him.

'I don't want this to end up in court,' a bald guy with thick eyebrows told him.

'Me neither,' Miron conceded. 'It's always better to settle things amicably.'

'Just remember I don't do night shifts,' a Botox-lipped bleach-blonde announced.

'So what do you expect? That everyone else will do night shifts, except you?' Miron grumbled back.

'Gabi asked me to tell you he's sorry,' said a man with rotting teeth and an earring.

'If he really was sorry,' Miron countered, 'he should have come and told me himself. No middlemen!'

'In your email you sounded taller,' a skinny redhead complained. 'In your email you sounded less picky,' Miron snapped.

And somehow everything worked out in the end. He and Baldy settled out of court. Botox Lips agreed to ask her sister to babysit so she could do one night shift a week. Rotting Teeth promised Gabi would phone, and the redhead and Miron agreed they weren't quite right for each other. Sometimes they paid the bill, sometimes he did. With the redhead, they split it. And it was all so fascinating, that if a whole morning went by when nobody sat down opposite him at the table, Miron felt let down. Luckily, this didn't happen too often.

Almost two months had gone by since the sweaty fat guy when a pockmarked man walked in. Despite the pocked face and the fact that he looked at least ten years older than Miron, he was good-looking with loads of charisma. The first thing he said as he sat down was: 'I was sure you wouldn't turn up.'

'But we agreed to meet,' Miron answered.

'Yes,' said the pockmarked man with a sad smile, 'except that after the way I shouted at you on the phone, I was afraid you'd chicken out.'

'So here I am,' Miron said, almost teasingly.

'I'm sorry I shouted at you on the phone,' the man apologised. 'Really, I just lost it. But I meant every word I said – got it? I'm asking you to stop seeing her.'

'But I love her,' Miron said in a choked voice.

'Sometimes you can love something but you still have to give it up,' the pockmarked man said. 'Listen to someone a little older than you. Sometimes you have to give it up.'

'Sorry,' Miron said, 'but I can't.'

'Yes, you can,' the man shot back. 'You can and you will. There's no other way. Maybe we both love her, but I happen to be her husband, and I'm not about to let you break up my family. Got that?'

Miron shook his head. 'You have no idea what my life has been like this past year,' he told the husband. 'Hell. Not even hell, just one great big stale chunk of nothing. And when you've been living with nothing for so long and suddenly something turns up, you can't just tell it to go away. You understand me, don't you? I know you understand me.'

The husband bit his lower lip. 'If you see her one more time,' he said, 'I'll kill you. I'm serious, and you know it.'

'So kill me,' Miron shrugged. 'That doesn't scare me. We're all going to die in the end.'

The husband leaned across the table and socked Miron in the jaw. It was the first time in his life that anyone had hit him so hard, and Miron felt a hot wave of pain surge up somewhere in the middle of his face and spread in every direction. Seconds later, he found himself on the floor, with the husband standing over him.

'I'll take her away from here,' the husband kept shouting, as he went on kicking Miron in the stomach and ribs. 'I'll take her far away, to another country, and you won't know where she is. You'll never see her again, you got that, you fucking piece of shit?'

Two waiters jumped on the husband and managed somehow to yank him away from Miron. Somebody yelled to the barman to call the police.

With his cheek still glued to the coolness of the floor, Miron watched the husband run out of the cafe. One of the waiters bent over and asked him if he was OK, and Miron made an attempt to answer.

'Do you want me to call an ambulance?' the waiter asked.

Miron whispered that he didn't. 'Are you sure?' the waiter insisted. 'You're bleeding.' Miron nodded slowly and shut his eyes. He tried as hard as he could to imagine himself with that woman. The one he'd never see again. He tried, and for a moment he almost succeeded. His whole body ached. He felt alive.

Teamwork

My son wants me to kill her. He's still young and doesn't express this perfectly just yet, but I know exactly what he's after. 'I want that Daddy to hit her hard,' he says.

'Hard so that she cries?' I ask him.

'No,' he says, turning his little head from side to side, 'even harder.'

He's not violent, my son. He's nearly four and a half, and I can't remember him ever asking me to hit anyone. He's also not the kind of child who goes around asking for things he doesn't need, like a rucksack with Dora on it or an ice-cream. He asks only when he feels he deserves it. Like his father.

And, if it's all right to point fingers, then *not* like his mother. Back in the day, she'd roll into the house with tears in her eyes and some story about a man who'd sworn at her on the motorway or ripped her off at the shops. I'd ask her to go over the facts in three or four different ways, ask questions, investigate, down to the tiniest details. Ninety per cent of the time it was clear she was at fault. That the man in the car was right to swear at her, and the one at the shop – all he did was add the sales tax to her bill.

But my little Roiki isn't like her. And if he asks his father to hit harder than to make her cry, I know there's really something going on. 'What did she do to you?' I ask. 'Did she hit you?'

'No,' Roiki says. 'When Mummy goes out, she babysits me. She locks the door with a key. She leaves me in my room in the dark and won't open it. Even if I cry. Even if I promise to be a good boy.'

I hug him tight-tight. 'Don't worry,' I tell him, 'Daddy will make it so Grandma stops.'

'You'll hit her harder than hard?' he asks me through his tears.

It's just heartbreaking to see your son cry. Even more so when you're divorced. And it fills me with a deep urge to answer Roi with a 'Yes', to swear that I will. But I don't say anything. I'm careful.

Because the absolute worst is promising something to a child and not seeing it through. An experience like that scars for life. I change the subject straight away. I say to him, 'Do you want to go to the car park at Daddy's work and I'll put you up on my lap and we'll drive the car together – teamwork style?'

As I say 'teamwork' his eyes light up, shining with excitement, and the tears that remain from before make them shine even brighter. We drive like that for maybe half an hour in the car park, him turning the wheel and me working the pedals. I even let him change the gears. Reverse cracks him up the most. There's nothing like the laughter of a child.

I bring him back fifteen minutes early. I know they're keeping an eye on us, so I'm extra careful about those things. Before we go up in the lift I check him twice over to make sure he's looking polished, that I'm delivering him dirt- and stain-free. Then I give myself the once over in the lobby mirror, checking for the same things.

'Where were you?' she asks before we're even through the door. 'At Gymboree,' Roiki answers – exactly as we agreed. 'We played with children.'

'I hope this time Daddy played nicely,' Sheyni says, looking all pleased with herself, 'and didn't push any children around.'

'Daddy didn't push anyone,' I say in a tone that makes it clear I'm not pleased she's baiting me in front of the boy.

'He didn't,' Roiki says. 'We had a lot of fun!'

He's completely forgotten his crying after the playground, and that he asked me to hurt Grandma. That's what's great about kids. Do with them what you will, an hour later they've forgotten all about it and they've found something else to think about, something good to be happy with. But I'm not a kid any more, and when I get back to the car all I've got in my head is a picture of Roiki in his tiny room, banging on the door, and that old sour mother of Sheyni's on the other side, not opening it. I have to be clever about this. I need to make sure it stops – but without putting myself in danger and jeopardising my visits with my son. Even these pathetic bi-weeklies cost me in blood.

I'm still paying for that one non-incident in the park. A little fat girl attacked Roi in the rope bridge section. She was pinching him hard and I was just trying to get her away from him. I gave her what is like the absence of a yank, barely pulling at her with my left hand, and the girl – she falls and bangs herself on the metal frame. Nothing, not a scratch, not even enough to get her clearly hysterical mother making a scene. But when Roiki mentions this to Sheyni by accident, she and Amram are suddenly crawling all over me like locusts. Sheyni says if I have a another 'violent outburst' in front of the child, the two of them will make sure the agreement we signed finds its way back to court for appeal.

'What violence?' I say to her. 'We were together five years, did I ever once raise a hand?' She knows she's got nothing to say on that front. She had it coming to her a shedload of times, and I was a picture of restraint. A different man would have kicked her straight into A & E at Ichilov. But me, on my life I'd never raise my hand against a woman. And somehow, before I know it, Amram's gone and got himself involved. 'Even now, right this minute, you're violent,' is what he throws out at me. 'You – you've got a crazy look in your eyes.'

'It's not a crazy look,' I say, and I smile at him. 'It's a touch of the human soul. It's what we call feeling. Just because you have no trace of it in you doesn't mean it's a bad thing.'

In the end, springing from the abundance of his non-violence, it's Amram who starts with the shouting, and the threats, telling me I'll never see my own son again. It's a shame I didn't record him. What a mouth that man cracked open, filthy as a sewer. But I keep smiling and acting all relaxed just to wind him up. We ended up settling the matter with me promising not to do anything like that ever again. As if it was just exactly what I had arranged for the next day, to find myself another five-year-old girl to knock down in the park.

Next time I pick up Roiki from the playground, I get straight to the subject of his grandma. I could wait, let him bring it up himself, but children will sit on those kinds of things for a long time, and that's time I don't have. 'Since our last talk,' I say, 'has Grandma come to babysit?'

Roiki licks the watermelon ice lolly I bought him and shakes his head. 'If she does it again,' he asks, 'are you going to make Grandma hurt?'

I breathe in. I want more than anything in the world to say yes, but I just can't risk it. If they make it so I can't see him any more, I'd die. 'I want to – more than anything,' I tell him. 'More than anything in the world, I want to hurt her. To hit her harder than hard. And not just Grandma. The same for anyone who hurts you.'

'Like that girl in ice-cream-cone park?' he says, his eyes sparkling.

'Like with the girl from the park,' I nod. 'But Mummy doesn't like it when Daddy hits. And if Daddy hits Grandma or anyone else, they won't let me come and play with you any more. To do all the things we do. Understand?'

Roiki doesn't answer. His lolly drips on his trousers. He lets it melt down on purpose, waiting for me to intervene. But I don't. After a long silence, he says, 'It's not nice for me alone in the room.'

'I know,' I tell him, 'but I can't make it stop. Only you can. And Daddy wants to teach you how.'

I explain to Roiki exactly what to do if his granny locks him in again. Which part of the head he needs to butt against the wall if he wants to leave a solid mark without really injuring himself.

'And it'll hurt?' he asks.

I tell him that it will. I'll never once in this life

lie to him. Not like Sheyni. When we were still together, we took Roi to the pediatrician for his vaccinations. The whole way there she was messing with his head, talking about stings and bees and special treats for good boys, right up until I cut her off mid-sentence and said, 'There's going to be a lady there with a needle who's going to cause you pain – but there's nothing we can do about it. There are some things in this world we just have to get on with.' And Roiki, who was then barely two, looked at me with that intelligent gaze of his and understood. When we got into the room you could see his whole being wanted to draw back. But he didn't protest and didn't run for the door. He took it like a little man.

Together, we go over every step of the plan. We run through the things he needs to tell Sheyni afterwards. How he annoyed Grandma. How she gave him a good shove into the wall. In short, how he got himself that bruise.

'And it'll hurt?' he asks again at the end.

'It'll hurt,' I tell him. 'Just this once. But afterwards, she'll never, not ever, shut you up in that room alone.'

Roiki goes quiet. He thinks. The ice lolly is

already finished. He's licking the stick. 'And Mummy won't say that I'm just making it up?'

I stroke his forehead. 'If there's a big enough bruise on your head, then, no, she won't say that.' After that, we take the car back to the car park. Roiki steers, and I press on the accelerator and the brake. Teamwork. I teach Roiki how to honk the horn while we drive, and he loves it. He honks and honks and honks until the car-park attendant comes over and asks us to stop. It's this old Arab who does the night shift. 'Please,' I say, winking and holding out a twenty. 'The boy's playing. A few more minutes and we'll be off.' The Arab doesn't say anything. He takes the money and heads back towards his booth.

'What did the man want?' Roiki asks.

'Nothing,' I tell him. 'He didn't understand where the noise was coming from.'

'And I can beep again?'

'Of course you can, angel.' I give him a kiss. 'More than once. Again and again. Honk until your heart's content.'

Pudding

The whole incident with Avishai Abudi should, in my opinion, set a red light flashing for us all. You'd be hard pressed to find a more ordinary guy. He's not the type to go around kicking over dustbins or starting fights in bars. In fact, he never does anything to draw attention to himself. And yet, one day, out of nowhere, a pair of thugs are banging at his door. They drag him down the stairs, stick him in the back of some van, and haul him straight to his parents' place. This, with a terrified Avishai in the back yelling, 'Who are you? What do you want?'

'That's not what you should be asking,' the driver says, and the brute at his side is nodding. 'What you mean to say is, "Who am I?" And, "What do I want?"' Afterwards the two of them laugh as if Avishai's just told the best joke in the world.

'I'm Avishai Abudi!' Avishai says in a tone intended to sound threatening. 'And I want to talk to your superiors. Do you hear me?' That's when the two of them park the van outside Avishai's parents' building and turn to face him. He's sure they're going to hit him and, also, that he doesn't deserve it. Not at all. 'You're in deep,' Avishai says, careful to protect his face. 'You guys have messed up, big time!' he says, as they pull him out of the van.

But the truth is, they don't beat him at all. Avishai can't see exactly what they're up to, but he senses it. And what he senses is that they are stripping his clothes from him, but not in a sexual way, it's all very proper. After they've finished dressing him back up, they put some sort of heavy pack on his back, and say, 'Hurry up, run along home to Mummy and Daddy. You wouldn't want to be late.' And Avishai runs. He runs as fast as he possibly can. He takes the stairs three at a time, until he reaches the brown wooden door to his parents' flat. He knocks on it, panting, and when Mummy opens the door, he hurries inside, closes it behind him and double-locks it. 'What's got into you?' Mummy asks. 'Why are you sweating like that?'

'I ran,' Avishai pants. 'On the stairs. People. Don't open.'

'I don't understand a thing,' Mummy says, 'but never mind. Come, put your bag down and go and wash your hands and face. Lunch is already on the table.' Avishai takes off the back pack, goes into the bathroom and washes his face. In the mirror over the sink he sees that he's in his school uniform. When he opens his bag in the living room he discovers notebooks and textbooks lined in flowered paper. There's a maths book, and a box of coloured pencils, and a little metal compass with a rubber shoved on the point. His mother comes over to chivvy him. 'This isn't the time for homework. Come and eat. Hurry up, chop-chop, before all the vitamins escape from the salad.' Avishai sits at the table and eats in silence. The food is delicious. He'd been surviving solely on takeaways and cheap restaurants for so many years, he'd honestly forgotten that food could taste this good. 'Daddy left you money for your after-school club.' Mummy points to a sealed white envelope resting on the little hall table next to the phone. 'But I'm warning you, Avi, if you pull the same stunt you did with the model-aeroplane club and change your mind after one session, you're better off telling us now, before we pay.'

Avishai thinks to himself: It's just a dream. And after that he says, 'Yes, Mummy,' because even if it is just a dream, there's no need to be impolite. He thinks to himself: If I just will it, I can wake myself at any moment. Not that he knows what exactly you do to wake up in the middle of a dream. You can pinch yourself, but that's generally used in the opposite situation. Pinching is what you do to prove you're already awake. Maybe he could hold his breath, or just say to himself, 'Wake up! Wake up!' And maybe if he simply refuses to absorb everything around him, if he casts doubt, it'll all suddenly melt away. In either case, there's no need to stress. He might as well eat first. Yes, after lunch is probably an excellent time to wake himself up. And when Avishai really gets to thinking about it, even when he's finished eating, it's not exactly urgent. He can go to his after-school club first – he's honestly curious which one it is – and later, if it's still light out, he can play football in the school playground. And only when Daddy gets home from work, only then will he wake up. He could even stretch it out another day or two, until just before some especially hard exam. 'Now what are you daydreaming about?' Mummy asks, stroking his balding head. 'So many thoughts spinning around behind those big, round eyes of yours, just looking at them makes me feel tired.'

'I was thinking of dessert,' Avishai lies, 'wondering if you'd made jelly or chocolate pudding.'

'What would you like there to be?' Mummy asks.

'Pudding,' Avishai says, all playful.

'It's ready,' his mother says happily and opens the fridge. 'But if you change your mind, jelly is just as easy. It won't take a minute to make.'

Actually, I've Had Some
Phenomenal Hard-Ons Lately

When Ronel woke up that magical Tuesday morning and found his beloved terrier, Darko, between his legs licking his morning erection, a single razor-sharp thought passed through his dull and relatively unoccupied brain: 'Is this sexual?' In other words, was Darko licking his penis the same way he licked Schneider's penis – Schneider being the miniature schnauzer Darko tried to have sexual intercourse with every time they bumped into each other in Meir Park – or was Darko licking his master's penis for the same reason he licked the dewdrops off a fragrant leaf? It was a troubling question, though not as troubling as the question of whether Neeva, his wide-hipped wife, suspected him of sleeping with his business partner, Renana, which would explain why she was so nasty to her on the phone, or was that sheer dislike? 'Oh, Darko, Darko,' Ronel muttered with a mixture of self-pity and affection, 'you're the only one who really loves me.' Darko may not have recognised a human male sex organ as such, but he always recognised his name, and he responded with a joyful bark. Clearly, it was better to be a dog coping with dog-dilemmas like the what-tree-should-I-pee-on-this-morning one, than to be Ronel grappling with such tedious moral quandaries as whether fucking Renana as she bent over his wife's dressing table was less repellent than fucking her right in their queen-size bed. A question that had many implications, by the way. Because if it didn't matter, they'd be a lot more comfortable doing it on the bed, and that would be that. Or, for example, whether fantasising about his naked wife while penetrating Renana offset the infidelity somewhat, or whether it was just another perversion. 'Daddy's not a pervert, Darko honey,' Ronel said as he stretched and got out of bed, 'Daddy's a complex person.' 'What?' Neeva asked, peering into the bedroom, 'Did you say something?' 'I told Darko I'd be home late because I have a meeting with the Germans tonight,' Ronel said, making the most of the rare eye contact with his wife. 'Oh, really?' Neeva sneered, 'And what did Darko have to say about that?' 'Nothing,' Ronel said, putting on a pair of grey pants, 'Darko accepts me.' 'Darko also accepts Purina dog food,' Neeva snapped. 'His standards aren't exactly high.'

One obvious advantage of having an affair with a colleague was that all those romantic candlelight dinners were tax deductible. It wasn't the only bonus, of course, but it was undoubtedly the one Ronel enjoyed most, because he never felt more relaxed and at peace than when he was stapling receipts to pieces of paper embellished with details and dates in his own handwriting. And when the receipt wasn't just his ticket to a tax deduction but an emotionally charged object in its own right, one that allowed him to reminisce about a night of successful lovemaking, the pleasure it gave him was doubled. 'I need a receipt for my tax', he said to the waiter, stressing the word 'tax', as if there were more than one kind of receipt in this little world of ours. The waiter nodded at Ronel as if to say he knew the score. Ronel didn't like him. Maybe because of the niggling way he corrected their pronunciation when they ordered, or maybe because he'd insisted on hiding his left arm behind his back throughout the whole meal, which made Ronel nervous. Or maybe it was just because he was a waiter who earned his living from tips, a form of payment that irritated Ronel because it had no place in the cosy womb of 'deductible expenses'. 'What's with you tonight?' Renana asked after they'd decided to abandon a failed attempt at wild sex in favour of watching the shopping channel together and eating watermelon. 'I'm stressed,' Ronel said. 'Stressed and a little weak, physically.' 'You were stressed last time too. And on Thursday, we didn't even try. Tell me . . .' She stopped speaking in order to swallow an especially large piece of watermelon, and as he waited out the lengthy process of her swallowing, Ronel knew he was in for some hassle. And in fact, a belch later, Renana picked up right where she'd left off. '. . . do you still fuck your wife or can't you do it with her either?' 'What do you mean, "either"?' Ronel said. Now he was annoyed. 'What, to be more precise, do you mean by "can't do it with her either"? Is there something we don't do?' 'Fuck,' Renana said, licking her stubby fingers. 'We don't fuck. Not that it's a big deal or anything. It's just that, when you're "a fuck on the side" and the whole sex thing stops, then you're nothing but "on the side", know what I mean? I'm not saying it's a deal breaker or anything, it's just, you know, a little weird. Because with your wife, even if you don't fuck, you can still visit her parents or fight about who loads the dishwasher, all the normal couple things. But when it happens with a lover, it sort of pulls the rug out.' 'Who said we don't fuck?' 'Your prick,' Renana said without a hint of provocation in her voice. 'That's why I asked about your wife, you know, to see if it's because I don't turn you on any more. Or if it's something more . . .' 'More what?' Ronel insisted as the pause lengthened. 'Give me a sec,' Renana mumbled, 'I'm looking for a gentler word than "impotent".' 'You're making a big deal over nothing,' Ronel said, getting angry. 'Just because once or twice I was a little bit tired and stressed out over work, it doesn't mean I'm impotent. I had a hard-on just this morning. Not an ordinary hard-on, either. It was phenomenal.' Ronel, remembering Darko, felt his organ stiffen a little, and for no reason, was filled with guilt. 'Terrific,' Renana said. 'That's good news. And who got to share this phenomenal hard-on of yours, Neeva?' 'No,' Ronel said,

momentarily confused, 'I shared it with myself.'
'How nice for you.' Renana smiled her famous
carrion-eating smile, which he'd previously come
across only at work, and went back to licking the
watermelon juice off the palm of her hand.

Even so, the night could conceivably have ended
with a fuck. Not a passionate fuck, but an angry
one, with Ronel trying to work up some desire
and have an erection, if only to make Renana eat
her words. Maybe. Who knows. But Ronel's mobile
vibrated in his shirt pocket right where his heart
should have been and brought the evening to a
new low. 'Sorry to disturb you in the middle of
your meeting with the Germans,' he heard Neeva's
hate-filled voice stretching out the word 'Germans'
as if she were referring to Hitler himself. 'Don't
be silly, sweetheart, you're not disturbing me at
all. We just finished,' Ronel said, sucking up to
Neeva the way he always did around clients. To
sound more credible, he even tossed a few words
in English at Renana. 'It's my wife. She says hello.'
Renana promptly gave a loud belch in reply. 'Mr
Mattenklott says hello, too,' Ronel said, afraid
Neeva might have heard her repulsive belch, and
added quickly, 'I think he's had one too many. I'll

just drop him and Ingo at the hotel and come home.' 'Ronel,' Neeva rebuked him on the other end of the line, 'I didn't call to find out when you're coming home. I called to tell you something.' 'I know, I know. I'm sorry,' Ronel apologised automatically as he tried to grab the remote from Renana, who was raising the volume. 'It's your dog,' Neeva added after a short silence. 'He ran away.'

When a dog takes a thin little saw and saws through the bars on the bathroom window, then shimmies down a few tied-together sheets, you can say, 'The dog ran away.' But when you're walking down the street with him and he's not on a lead, and an hour later you realise he's nowhere to be seen, we're talking about a personal screw-up. Trying to put the blame on Darko wasn't fair. 'He was probably sniffing a kerb or a pillar and when he looked up, he realised you weren't there,' he said to Neeva in an accusing tone as they walked down King George Street trying to reconstruct the route of that disastrous evening stroll. 'How many times have I told you not to let him out of your sight?' 'Tell me,' Neeva said as she stopped walking and stood in the middle of the street like a wife about to make a scene, 'what exactly are you trying to say? That I'm not a good enough babysitter for your smelly dog? That I don't walk him according to the rules of the International Dog Walkers Association? If you were at home instead of fucking around with your Germans, you could've taken him out yourself and none of this would have happened.' Ronel could have complained about how he worked his arse off till all hours just to put food on the table, but decided, for tactical reasons, to keep quiet. One of the first things he'd learned in the world of business was never to reach a point of no return. You should always leave as many options open as possible. This often means not saying or doing the thing you wanted to say or do. Now, for example, he felt very much like kicking Neeva in the shin as hard as he could. Not only because she'd let Darko run away, but also because she didn't call him by his name and insisted on referring to him as 'smelly', and mainly because she refused to take responsibility for her actions and behaved as if this terrible tragedy were God's way of punishing Ronel and not her own self-centred, irresponsible mistake. He didn't kick her in the shin as hard as he could because that, as already mentioned, would have been a point of no return. Instead, with the same composure and self-control so often displayed by murderers when cleaning up the scene of the crime and getting rid of their victims' bodies, Ronel suggested that she go home and wait there in case someone called with information about Darko. 'Who's going to call?' Neeva laughed. 'Your stupid dog from a payphone? Or his kidnappers asking for a ransom? Even if someone does find him, they won't know our phone number.' 'I still think it would be better if we split up,' Ronel insisted and seriously considered abandoning the insight that had served him so well for so many years and kicking her very hard in the shins after all. When she persisted in asking why, he shook his head wildly and said, 'No reason.'

Ronel leaned against a yellow post box and read the list he'd just made on the back of the receipt from the restaurant he and Renana had eaten in that night. The list was headed 'Places Darko Likes (?)' He didn't know why he'd tacked on the question mark and parentheses. Maybe because he felt that if the list didn't include an element of uncertainty, it would be like claiming he knew all there was to know about Darko, whereas Ronel himself had readily admitted countless times, to himself and to others, that he didn't always understand Darko. Why he sometimes barked and other times chose not to. Why he started digging holes so furiously, then left the excavation as suddenly as he'd began, for no obvious reason. Did he think of Ronel as his master? His father? His friend? Maybe even as his lover?

The first place on the list was Meir Park, where he and Darko went every morning. That was where Darko met the dogs who were his friends and enemies, not to mention his bosom buddy, the stumpy Schneider. At that late hour, there were neither dogs nor people in Meir Park. Only a drunk, homeless Russian, dozing on a bench. Ronel presumed he was Russian not just because of the somewhat stereotypical bottle of vodka cradled in his arms, but because he kept laughing and speaking Russian in his sleep. Ronel stopped for a minute and said to himself that despite the troubles that kept plaguing him and sometimes made him feel like a latter-day Job, or at least a Job-lite, he should be grateful for what he had and thank whoever it is non-religious people thank about such things for not putting him in that Russian man old, torn, newspaper-stuffed shoes. The Russian's laughter grew deeper and louder, crushing Ronel's certainty of his own happiness. 'Who says?' Ronel asked, suddenly filled with a great truth diluted by a substantial amount of self-pity, 'Who says my fate is better than his? Here I am in the same park as him. He's drunk and happy. And I'm neither. All I have in the world is a dog who's abandoned me, a wife I don't really love, and a business . . .' The thought of his business cheered him up a little. This was, after all, a period of growth. Not that that promised boundless joy, but still, for now, it was preferable to newspaper in his shoes.

Near the park exit, Ronel noticed a rapid dog-like movement in the bushes. But after a closer inspection, he saw that the object of his shattered hope was the short, bearded shadow of Schneider. Ronel, who frequented the park only during the day, was surprised to see Schneider there so late at night. His first thought was that some sixth sense had told Schneider that Darko was lost and he'd left his house to join the search, but a familiar whistle punctured that heroic version of events.

And right after that whistle came Alma, Schneider's beautiful, limping mistress. Alma, who was about twenty-five, was one of the most beautiful women Ronel knew, and definitely the lamest. She'd been injured in an unusually stupid car accident, and had used the money she received in settlement to buy a fully renovated penthouse on Michal Street. Alma's extreme encounter with a bad driver and an excellent lawyer (she'd even told Ronel his name once, but since there were no injury claims on his horizon, he quickly forgot it) had undoubtedly shifted the course of her life. People always say they would pass up any amount of money to get their health back, but was that really true? Alma, as far as he could tell from a lead away, always smiled a genuine-looking smile, which Ronel had tried to imitate for business purposes. He had even practised a few times in front of the mirror before he gave up and opted for an easier version. Hers was a permanent smile that rested on her face, a default smile, not fixed or phoney, always in tune with whatever was happening around it – broadening, narrowing, turning surprised or cynical when called for, but always there and always relaxed. It was the relaxation of that smile that

made Ronel try to imitate it, recognising its supe-
riority as a negotiating tool over any other expression. Would she have smiled that way if she were
poor and had a platinum-free leg? Or would the
smile have been different, less serene? More fright-
ened by an uncertain economic future, by the
threat of old age looming over her perfect beauty?
'I didn't know you and Darko came here at night,'
Alma said, hopping into the shaft of light at the
entrance to the park. 'We don't,' Ronel groaned
desperately. 'Darko ran away,' he said, but quickly
corrected himself, 'I mean he got lost.' Schneider
was looking all around Ronel with the annoying
friskiness of a stupid and not particularly sensitive
schnauzer. 'He doesn't understand,' Alma apologised. 'He smells Darko on your clothes and thinks
he's here.' 'I know, I know,' Ronel said nodding,
and for no reason, burst into tears. 'But he's not.
He's not here. He could be dead by now. Run
over. Or maybe some kids are torturing him in a
park somewhere, putting out cigarettes on him,
or maybe the city dog-catchers got him . . .' Alma
put a comforting hand on his arm, and even
though her hand was damp with sweat, there
was something pleasant about that dampness,

something gentle and alive. 'Dog-catchers don't work at night, and Darko's a clever dog. There's no way he was run over. If it were Schneider . . .' she said, giving her lively schnauzer the kind of sad, loving look beautiful girls always save for their ugly friends, 'then we'd have to worry. But Darko knows how to take care of himself. I can just see him whining outside the entrance to your building. Or on your doormat right now, chewing on a stolen bone.'

Even though he could have called Neeva to ask whether Darko had come back, Ronel decided to go home. It was close by, and anyway, now that Alma had managed to convince him that Darko might be there, he didn't want Neeva to be the one to tell him the good news. 'She and I,' he thought, 'should have separated a long time ago.' Once, he remembered, he'd looked at Neeva when she was sleeping and imagined a horrible scenario in which she died in a terrorist attack. He'd be sorry for cheating on her and he'd cry live on the six o'clock news out of guilt cunningly disguised as pure grief. That thought, he now remembered, had been sad and terrible, but, to his surprise, it had also made him feel a kind of relief. As if her being wiped out of his life might open up a space for something else, something with colours and smells and vividness. But before he could feel guilty again about this sensation of relief, Renana had made her entrance into the scenario and now that Neeva was no longer part of it, she had moved in with him right away, at first to comfort and support him in his hour of need. Then she'd just stayed. Ronel remembered how he'd gone on and on in his imagination, till he had reached the point when Renana had said, 'It's me or Darko.' He had chosen Darko and remained alone in his flat. Without a woman. Without love, except for Darko's, whose existence only intensified the terrible loneliness he called his life. 'Terrorism is awful,' Ronel had thought that night. 'It destroys life in an instant,' and he had given Neeva's sleeping forehead a gentle kiss.

Ronel almost walked past Darko without noticing him. He was too busy trying to find a lighted window in his third-floor flat. Darko was busy too, his filmy glance admiringly following the quick hands of the owner of Tarboosh Shwarma as they cut thin slices of meat from the revolving spit. But when the two friends finally spotted each other, their reunion was filled with lavish face-licking and emotion. 'That's some dog,' the shwarma guy said as he kneeled in front of Darko, placing a piece of paper with a few greasy slices of meat on the pavenent like a high priest making a sacrifice to his god. 'I want you to know that a lot of dogs come here, and I don't give them anything. But this one . . .' he said, pointing at Darko. 'Tell me, does he happen to be Turkish?' 'What do you mean, Turkish?' Ronel asked, offended. 'Oh, nothing,' the shwarma guy apologised. 'I'm from Izmir, so I thought . . . When I was a boy, I had a dog just like him, a puppy. But he used to pee in the house, which drove my mother mad, so she threw him out, like he did it on purpose. But you, you're a good man. He ran away from you and you're not even cross. Believe me, that's how it should be. I don't understand all those tough guys who clobber their dogs with the lead if they stop for a minute to watch the shwarma turn. What are they, Nazis?' 'He didn't run away,' Ronel corrected him as he pressed his tired forehead against Darko's sturdy back, 'he got lost.'

That night, Ronel decided to write a book, something between an educational fable and a philosophical treatise. The story would be about a king beloved by all his subjects who loses something he cherishes, not money, maybe a child or something, or a nightingale, if nobody'd used that yet. Around page one hundred, the book would turn into something less symbolic and more modern that dealt with man's alienation in contemporary society and offered a little consolation. On about page one hundred and sixty or seventy, it would change into a kind of airport novel in terms of readability, but of much higher quality. And on page three hundred, the book would turn into a furry little animal readers could hug and stroke, as a way of coping with their loneliness. He hadn't yet decided on what sort of technology would turn the book into that ever-so-touchable animal, but he made a note to himself before he fell asleep that in the last few years, both molecular biology and publishing had taken giant steps forward and were now crying out to join forces.

And that same night, Ronel had a dream, and in his dream he was sitting on the balcony of his

house concentrating on the newspaper in a coura-
geous and sincere effort to solve the enigma of
human existence. His beloved dog, Darko, suddenly
appeared on the balcony wearing a grey suit, a
giant bone in his mouth. He put the bone down
at his feet and hinted to Ronel with a tilt of his
head that he should look for the answer in the
financial pages. Then he explained in a deep,
human voice, which sounded a little like Ronel's
father's voice, that the human race is nothing but
a tax dodge. 'A tax dodge?' Ronel repeated,
confused. 'Yes,' Darko nodded his clever head. He
explained to Ronel that his tax consultant, an
extraterrestrial who lived on the planet Darko
originally came from, had advised him to invest
his earnings in an ecologically orientated enter-
prise, because ecology was big with the extraterrestrial tax department. And that, using shell
corporations, he soon got involved in the whole
field of developing life and species on planets. 'In
general,' Darko explained, 'everyone knows there's
no real money in developing the human race. Or
any other race, for that matter. But since it's a new
field that's wide open taxationally, there's nothing
to stop me from submitting a mountain of receipts.'

'I don't believe it,' Ronel said in his dream. 'I refuse to believe that our only function in this world is to be a tax shelter so my beloved dog can launder money.' 'First of all,' Darko corrected him, 'no one's talking about money laundering here. All my revenue's clean and above board, I don't do any of that funny business. All we're talking about here is a semi-legitimate inflation of expenses. Now, secondly, let's say I grant your first premise that it isn't humanity's real function to be a tax shelter for me, OK? If we take this argument a little further, what other function could it have? I'm not asking pragmatically, but theoretically.' Darko kept quiet for a little while, and when he saw Ronel didn't have a single answer in his arsenal, he barked twice, picked up the bone with his mouth and left the balcony. 'Don't go,' Ronel begged in a whisper. 'Please, don't leave me, my dog, my friend, my love . . .'

That morning too, Ronel woke up to a glorious hard-on and Darko's indeterminate licking. When he finally opened his eyes. Darko was running around the room boneless and completely naked. 'It's not sexual,' was the first thought that came into Ronel's mind, 'it's sociable, maybe even existential.' 'Darko, my angel, my friend,' he whispered, trying to contain the overwhelming joy he felt so as not to wake Neeva, 'you're the only one who really loves me.'

Unzipping

It began with a kiss. It almost always begins with a kiss. Ella and Tsiki were in bed, naked, with only their tongues touching – when she felt something prick her. 'Did I hurt you?' Tsiki asked, and when she shook her head, he quickly added, 'You're bleeding.' And she was, from the mouth. 'I'm sorry,' he said and started a frantic search in the kitchen, pulling ice-cube trays out of the freezer and banging them against the worktop. 'Here, take these,' he said, handing her some ice with a shivering hand, 'put them against your lip. It'll stop the bleeding.' Tsiki had always been good at these things. In the army he'd been a paramedic. He was a trained tour guide too. 'I'm sorry,' he went on, turning paler, 'I must have bitten you. You know, in the heat of passion.' 'Never –ind,' she smiled at him, the ice cube sticking to her lower lip. 'No—ing ha—ened.' Which was a lie, of course. Because some—ing had ha—ened. It isn't every day that someone you're living with makes you bleed, and then lies to you and says he bit you, when you distinctly felt something pricking you.

They didn't kiss for a few days after that, because of her cut. Lips are a very sensitive part of the body. And later when they could, they had to be very careful. She could tell he was hiding something. And sure enough, one night, taking advantage of the fact that he slept with his mouth open, she gently slipped her finger under his tongue – and found it. It was a zip. A teensy zip. But when she pulled at it, her whole Tsiki opened up like an oyster, and inside was Jurgen. Unlike Tsiki, Jurgen had a goatee, meticulously shaped sideburns and an uncircumcised penis. Ella watched him in his sleep. Very, very quietly she folded up the Tsiki wrapping and hid it in the kitchen cupboard behind the rubbish bin, where they kept the bin bags.

Life with Jurgen wasn't easy. The sex was fantastic, but he drank a lot, and when he did, he'd make a racket and get into all kinds of embarrassing situations. On top of that, he liked to make her feel guilty for being the reason he'd left Europe and come to live here. Whenever anything bad happened in this country, whether it was in real life or on TV, he'd say to her, 'Look what your country is coming to.' His Hebrew was lousy, and that 'your' of his always sounded very accusatory. Her parents didn't like him. Her mother, who had actually been fond of Tsiki, called Jurgen the goy. Her father would always ask him about work, and Jurgen would snigger and say, 'Work is like a moustache, Mr Shviro. It went out of style a long time ago.' Which nobody ever found amusing, certainly not Ella's father, who still happened to sport a moustache.

Finally, Jurgen left. He went back to Düsseldorf to make music and live on benefits. He'd never be able to make it as a singer in this country, he said, because they'd hold his accent against him. People here were prejudiced. They didn't like Germans. Ella thought that even in Germany his weird music and kitschy lyrics wouldn't really get him very far. He'd even written a song about her. It was called 'Goddess' and the whole thing was about having sex on the breakwater and about how, when she came, it was 'like a wave breaking against a rock', – and that's a quote.

Six months after Jurgen left she was looking for a bin bag and found the Tsiki wrapping. Maybe it had been a mistake to undo his zip, she thought. Could be. With things like that it's hard to say for sure. That same evening, while she was brushing her teeth, she thought back over that kiss, over the pain of being pricked. She rinsed her mouth with lots of water and looked in the mirror. She still had a scar, and when she studied it up close, she noticed a little zip under her tongue. Ella fingered it hesitantly, and tried to imagine what she'd be like inside. It made her very hopeful, but also a bit worried – mainly about freckled hands and a dry complexion. Maybe she'd have a tattoo, she thought, of a rose. She'd always wanted to have one, but never had the nerve. She'd thought it would hurt a lot.

The Polite Little Boy

The polite little boy knocked on the door. His parents were too busy arguing to answer, and after he'd knocked a few times he went in anyway. 'A mistake,' the father said to the mother, 'that's what we are, a mistake, like in those pictures where they show you how not to do something. That's what we are, with a big "No!" underneath and the face crossed out with a big X.' 'What do you want me to say?' the mother said to the father. 'I mean, anything I say now I'll regret later.' 'Say it, say it,' the father snarled. 'Why wait till later when you can regret it right now?' The polite little boy had a model aeroplane in his hand. He'd built it himself. The instructions were in a language he didn't understand, but there were good drawings, with arrows, and the polite little boy, whose father always said he had good hands, managed to work them out and to build the model aeroplane, with no help from grown-ups. 'I used to laugh,' the mother said, 'I'd laugh a lot, every day. And now . . .' She stroked the polite little boy's hair distractedly. 'I don't any more, that's all.' 'That's all?' the father roared. 'That's all? That's your "I'll regret saying it later": "I used to laugh"? Big fucking deal!'

'What a nice plane,' the mother said and very deliberately turned her gaze away from the father. 'Why don't you go outside and play with it?' 'May I?' the polite little boy asked. 'Of course you may,' the mother smiled and stroked his hair again, the way you stroke a dog's head. 'And how long may I stay outside?' the polite little boy asked. 'As long as you want,' the father blurted, 'and if you like it out there, you don't have to come back at all. Just pick up the phone from time to time, so Mother doesn't worry.' The mother got up, and slapped the father as hard as she could. It was strange, because it looked as if this slap only made the father happy, and it was actually the mother who started crying. 'Go on, go ahead,' the mother told the polite little boy between her sobs, 'go out and play, while there's still light outside, but be back before it gets dark.' 'Maybe his face is hard as a stone,' the polite little boy thought to himself as he walked down the stairs, 'and that's why it hurts your hand when you hit it.'

The polite little boy threw the model aeroplane in the air as high as he could. It made a loop, went on gliding a little in parallel with the ground, and bumped into a drinking fountain. The wing was slightly bent out of shape and the polite little boy tried hard to straighten it. 'Wow,' said a freckled-faced little girl he hadn't noticed until then, and held out her freckled hand. 'What a cool plane. Can I fly it too?' 'It isn't a plane,' the little boy corrected. 'It's a model aeroplane. A plane is only if it has a motor.' 'C'mon, let me try it,' the little girl ordered without lowering her hand. 'Don't be mean.' 'I have to fix the wing first,' the little boy stalled. 'Can't you see it's bent out of shape?' 'You're mean,' the little girl said. 'I hope lots of horrible things happen to you.' She wrinkled her forehead, trying to think of some-thing more specific, and when it came to her, she smiled. 'I hope your mummy dies. That's it, I hope she dies. Amen.' The polite little boy paid no attention to her, just as he'd been taught to do.

He was a head taller than the little girl and if he'd wanted to he could have slapped her, and it would have hurt the little girl a lot, much more than it would have hurt him, because her freckled face was definitely not made of stone. But he didn't, and he didn't kick her either, or throw a pebble, or say something horrible back to her, because he was polite. 'And I hope your daddy dies too,' the little girl added, as if it was an afterthought, and walked away.

The polite little boy flew the model aeroplane a few more times. On his best throw, it made three whole loops in the air before dropping to the ground. The sun was beginning to drop too, and the sky all around was getting redder and redder. His father had told him once that if you look at the sun for a very long time without blinking, you can go blind, and that's why the polite little boy was careful to close his eyes every few seconds. But even with his eyes closed, he could still see the redness of the sky. It was strange, and the polite little boy was very eager to understand it better, but he knew that unless he got home on time, his mother would worry. 'The sun always rises,' the polite little boy thought to himself, and bent over to pick up the model aeroplane off the lawn, 'and I'm never late.'

When the polite little boy went indoors, his mother was still in the living room crying, clutching her hand. The father wasn't there. She said he was in their bedroom, asleep, because he was doing a night shift, and she went to make the polite little boy his Scrambled Surprise supper. The bedroom door was ajar and the polite little boy gave it a gentle push. The father was lying on the bed with his shoes and his clothes on. He was on his stomach with his eyes open, and when the polite little boy peeked inside, he asked, without lifting his head up off the bed, 'How's the model aeroplane?' 'It's OK,' the polite little boy said, and when he felt that what he'd said wasn't enough, he added, 'It's really OK.' 'Mother and I fight sometimes and say things to hurt one another,' the father said, looking down at the floor and then at him, 'but you know that I'll always love you. Always. No matter what anyone says. Don't you?' 'Yes,' the polite little boy nodded, and started closing the door behind him. 'I know. Thank you.'

Mystique

The man who knew what I was about to
say sat next to me on the plane, a stupid smile
plastered across his face. That's what was so nerve-
racking about him, the fact that he wasn't clever
or even sensitive, and yet he knew the lines and
managed to say them – all the lines I meant to
say – three seconds before me. 'D'you sell Guerlain
Mystique?' he asked the stewardess a minute
before I could, and she gave him an orthodontic
smile and said there was just one last bottle left.
'My wife's obsessed with that perfume. It's like an
addiction with her. If I come back from a trip and
don't get a bottle of Mystique from duty-free, she
tells me I don't love her any more. If I dare walk
in the door without at least one bottle, I'm in
trouble.' That was supposed to be my line, but the
man who knew what I was about to say stole it

from me. He didn't miss a beat. As soon as the wheels touched down, he switched on his phone, a second before I did, and called his wife. 'I just landed,' he told her. 'I'm sorry. I know it was supposed to be yesterday. They cancelled the flight. You don't believe me? Check it yourself. Call Eric. I know you don't. I can give you his number right now.' I also have a travel agent called Eric. He'd lie for me too.

When the plane reached the gate he was still on the phone, giving all the answers I would have given. Without a trace of emotion, like a parrot in a world where time flows backwards, repeating whatever's about to be said instead of what's been said already. His answers were the best possible, under the circumstances. His circumstances weren't so hot, not so hot at all. Mine weren't all that great either. My wife hadn't taken my call yet, but just listening to the man who knew what I was about to say made me want to hang up. Just listening to him I could tell that the hole I was in was so deep that if I ever managed to dig myself out, it would be to a different reality. She'd never forgive me, she'd never trust me. Ever. From now on, every trip would be hell on earth, and the time in between would be even worse. He went on and on and on, delivering all those sentences that I'd thought up and hadn't said yet. They just kept flowing out of him. Now he stepped it up, raising his voice, like a drowning man desperate to stay afloat. People started filing out of the plane. He got up, still talking, scooped up his laptop in his other hand and headed for the exit. I could see him leaving it behind, the bag he'd stashed in the overhead compartment. I could see him forgetting it, and I didn't say anything. I just stayed put. Gradually, the plane emptied, till the only ones left were an overweight religious woman with a million children, and me. I got up and opened the overhead compartment, like it was the most natural thing in the world to do. I took out the duty-free bag, like it had always been mine. Inside were the receipt and the bottle of Guerlain Mystique. My wife's obsessed with that perfume. It's like an addiction with her. If I come back from a trip and don't get a bottle of Mystique from duty-free, she tells me I don't love her any more. If I dare walk in the door without at least one bottle, I'm in trouble.

Creative Writing

The first story Maya wrote was about a world in which people split themselves in two instead of reproducing. In that world, every person could, at any given moment, turn into two beings, each half his or her age. Some chose to do it when they were young; for instance, an eighteen-year-old might split into two nine-year-old girls. Others would wait until they'd established themselves professionally and financially and only went for it in middle age.

The heroine of Maya's story is splitless. She has reached the age of eighty, and despite all the social pressure, insists on not splitting. At the end of the story, she dies. It was a good story, except for the ending. There was something depressing about it. Depressing and predictable. But in the workshop Maya actually got a lot of compliments on the ending. The teacher, who was supposed to be a well-known writer or something, even though Aviad had never heard of him, told her there was something soul-piercing about the banality of the ending, or some other piece of crap. Aviad saw how happy that compliment made her. She was very excited when she told him about it. She recited what the writer had said to her the way people recite a verse from the Bible. And Aviad, who at first had tried to suggest a different ending, back-pedalled and said that it was all a matter of taste and that he really didn't understand much about it.

It was her mother's idea that she should go to a creative writing workshop. She'd said that a friend's daughter had gone to one last year and enjoyed it very much. Aviad also thought it would be good for Maya to get out more, to do something with herself. He could always bury himself in work, there was always something in the business he had to take care of. But she, since the miscarriage, never left the house. Whenever he came in he found her in the living room, sitting up straight. Not reading, not watching TV, not even crying. When Maya hesitated about the course, Aviad knew how to persuade her. 'Go once, give it a try,' he said, 'the way a child goes to day camp.' Later he thought it had been a little insensitive to use a child as an example after what they'd been through two months ago. But Maya actually smiled and said that day camp might be just what she needed.

The second story she wrote was about a world in which you could only see people you love. The protagonist was a married man in love with his wife. One day, his wife walks straight into him in the hallway and the glass he's holding falls and shatters on the floor. A few days later, she sits down on him as he's dozing in an armchair. Both times, she wriggles out of it with an excuse: she had something else on her mind; she'd been looking somewhere else when she'd sat down. But the husband starts suspecting that she doesn't love him any more. To test his theory, he decides to do something drastic and shaves off the left side of his moustache. He comes home with half a moustache, clutching a bouquet of anemones. His wife thanks him for the flowers and smiles. He can sense his wife groping the air as she tries to give him a kiss. Maya called that story 'Half a

Moustache', and told Aviad that when she read it aloud in the workshop, some people had cried. Aviad smiled at her and said, 'Wow,' and kissed her on the forehead. That night, they argued about some stupid little thing. She'd forgotten to pass on a message or something like that, and he'd shouted at her. He was to blame, and in the end, he apologised. 'I had a hellish day at work,' he said and stroked her leg, trying to make up for his outburst, 'Do you forgive me?' And she forgave him.

The creative writing teacher had published a novel and a collection of short stories. Neither was much of a success, but they did get a few good reviews. That's what the saleswoman at a bookshop near his office told Aviad. The novel was very thick, 624 pages. Aviad bought the book of short stories. He kept it in his desk and tried to read some during lunch breaks. All the stories in the collection took place abroad. It was a kind of gimmick. Each story was set in a different country. The blurb on the back cover said that the writer was a tour guide and had travelled the world. There was also a small black-and-white picture of him. In it, he had the kind of smug smile on his face of someone who feels lucky to be who he is.

The writer told her, Maya said to Aviad, that when the course was over, he'd send her stories to his editor. And while she shouldn't get her hopes up, for the past few years, publishers have been desperate for new talent.

Her third story started out funny. It was about a pregnant woman who gives birth to a cat. The hero of the story is the husband, who suspects that the cat isn't his. A fat, ginger tomcat that sleeps on the cover of the wheelie bin right opposite the couple's bedroom gives the husband a condescending look every time he goes downstairs to put out the rubbish. In the end, there's a violent clash between the husband and the cat. The husband throws a stone at the cat, who counters with bites and scratches. The injured husband, his wife and the kitten she's breastfeeding are waiting in the clinic for him to get a tetanus jab. He's humiliated and in pain, but tries not to cry. The kitten, sensing his suffering, curls out of its mother's embrace, goes over to him, licks his face tenderly and offers a consoling 'Miaow.'

'Did you hear that?' the mother asks emotionally. 'He said "Daddy."'

At that point, the husband can no longer hold

back his tears. And when he read that passage, Aviad had to try hard not to cry too. Maya said that she'd started writing that story even before she knew she was pregnant again. 'Isn't it weird,' she asked, 'how my brain didn't know I was pregnant yet, but my subconscious did?' The next Tuesday, when Aviad was supposed to pick her up after her class, he arrived half an hour early, parked his car and went to find her. Maya was surprised to see him in the classroom, and he insisted that she introduce him to the writer. The writer reeked of perfume. He shook Aviad's hand limply and told him that if Maya had chosen him for a husband, he must be a very special person.

Three weeks later, Aviad signed up for a beginners' creative writing class. He didn't say anything about it to Maya, and to be on the safe side, he told his secretary that if he had any calls from home, she should say he was in an important meeting and couldn't be disturbed. The other members of the class were elderly women, who gave him dirty looks. The thin, young teacher wore a headscarf, and the women in the class gossiped about her, saying that she lived in a settlement in the occupied territories and had cancer. She asked everyone to do an exercise in automatic writing. 'Write whatever comes into your head,' she said, 'don't think, just write.' Aviad tried to stop thinking. It was very hard. The old women around him wrote with nervous speed, like students trying to finish an exam before the teacher tells them to put their pens down, and after a few minutes, he began writing too. The story he wrote was about a fish that was swimming happily along in the sea when a wicked witch turned it into a man. The fish couldn't come to terms with the change and decided to chase down the wicked witch and make her turn him back into a fish. Since it was an especially quick and enterprising fish, it managed to get married while it was pursuing her, and even to establish a small company that imported plastic products from the Far East. With the help of the enormous knowledge he had gained as a fish that had crossed the seven seas, the company began to thrive, and at one point, even went public. Meanwhile, the wicked witch, who was a little tired of all her years of wickedness, decided to find everyone she'd cast a spell on, apologise to them and restore them to their natural state. At one point, she even went to see the fish she had turned into a man. The fish's secretary asked her to wait until he'd finished an international conference call with his partners in Taiwan. At that stage in its life, the fish could hardly remember that it was in fact a fish, and its company already controlled half the world. The witch waited several hours, and when she saw that the meeting didn't seem to be ending, she climbed onto her broom and flew off. The fish kept doing better and better, not to mention becoming busier and busier, until one day, when it was really old, it looked out of the window of one of the dozens of huge shoreline buildings it had purchased in a smart property deal, and saw the sea. And suddenly it remembered that it was a fish. A very rich fish that controlled dozens of subsidiary companies traded on stock markets around the world, but still a fish. A fish that, for years, had not tasted the salt of the sea. When the teacher saw that Aviad had stopped writing, she gave him an enquiring look. 'I don't have an ending,' he whispered apologetically, keeping his voice down so as not to disturb the old ladies who were still writing.

Snot

A father and son are sitting at a desk in an acupuncturist's treatment room, waiting.

The acupuncturist comes in.

He's Chinese.

He sits down behind the desk.

In strangely accented English, he asks the son to put his hands on the desk.

The Chinese acupuncturist puts his fingers on the son's arms and closes his eyes, then asks son to stick out his tongue.

The son sticks it out defiantly.

The Chinese acupuncturist nods and asks the son to lie down on the treatment bed.

The son lies down on the bed and closes his eyes.

The father asks if the son should take off his clothes.

The acupuncturist shakes his head.

He takes some long, thin needles out of his desk drawer and starts sticking them into the son.

One behind each ear.

One in each cheek, close to the nose.

One on each side of his forehead, close to the eye.

The son moans quietly, his eyes still closed.

Now, says the acupuncturist to father and son, we have to wait.

And after the treatment, asks the father, will he feel better?

The acupuncturist shrugs and walks out.

The father goes over to the bed and puts a hand on his son's shoulder.

The son's body contracts.

The son didn't flinch when his skin was being pierced by needles, but he does now. Half an hour later, the Chinese acupuncturist comes back and pulls each needle out with a swift movement.

He tells the father and the son that the boy's body is responding to the treatment, and that's a good sign.

As proof, he points to the spots where the

needles had been inserted. There is a red circle around each one.

Then he sits down behind the desk.

The father asks how much the treatment costs.

He'd planned to ask before the treatment, but forgot. If he'd remembered to ask earlier, he would have had a better bargaining position. Not that he planned to bargain. After all, we're talking about the health of his only son here. His only living son, that is.

The acupuncturist says three hundred and fifty shekels per treatment and then tells him that there is medication the son has to take after eating, and that costs another hundred.

The acupuncturist explains that the boy needs a series of treatments. At least ten. Every day except Saturday.

The acupuncturist adds that it would be better if they could do the treatment on Saturday too, but he doesn't work Saturdays because his wife won't let him.

'Wife' is almost the only word other than 'snot' that he says in Hebrew.

When he says 'wife', the father feels a terrible sense of loneliness.

Then the father has a strange idea.

He wants to tell the acupuncturist that he has to go to the loo and then, after locking the door behind him, he'll masturbate into the toilet.

He thinks this will bring him some relief from that sense of loneliness. He's not sure.

In Chinese medicine, sperm is considered a form of energy. When you ejaculate it, you are weakened, and that's why it isn't recommended. Especially when you're weak to begin with.

The father doesn't know any of that, but he gives up on the idea anyway. Loneliness is hard for him, but he doesn't feel comfortable leaving his son alone with the Chinese acupuncturist.

Every day except Saturday, the acupuncturist repeats. He thinks the father wasn't listening the first time.

The father pays with new notes. Exactly four hundred and fifty. No change necessary.

They make an appointment for the next day.

On the way to the door, the Chinese acupuncturist says in Hebrew, 'Be well, you two.'

The son thinks it's weird for the acupuncturist to say that. After all, he's the only one who's ill.

Suddenly, a Knock on the Door

The father doesn't notice it. He's thinking about something else.

'Wife', 'snot', 'be well, you two'.

'Be well, you two', 'snot', 'wife'.

There's nothing stranger than hearing a Chinese man speak Hebrew.

Grab the Cuckoo by the Tail

It's hardest at night. Don't get me wrong, though. I'm not saying I miss her most at night – because I don't miss her, full stop. But at night, when I'm alone in bed, I do think about her. Not warm, fuzzy thoughts about all the good times we had. More like a picture of her in knickers and a T-shirt, sleeping with her mouth open, breathing heavily, leaving a circle of saliva on the pillow, and of myself watching her. What did I actually feel then when I was watching her? First of all, amazement that I wasn't turned off, and after that, a sort of affection. Not love. Affection. The kind you feel towards an animal or a baby more than towards a wife. Then I cry. Almost every night. And not out of regret. I have nothing to regret. She's the one who left. And looking back, our splitting up was good, not just for her, for both of us. And it's even better that we did it before there were kids in the middle to make everything more complicated. So why do I cry? Because that's just how it is. When something gets taken away from you, even if it's shit, it hurts. When a tumour is removed, you're left with a scar. And the best time to scratch it seems to be at night.

Uzi has a new mobile phone, the kind that gets real-time updates from the stock market. When the stocks of his computer company go up, his phone plays 'Simply the Best', and when they go down, it plays 'Hard Rain is Going to Fall'. He's been walking around with that phone for a month now, and it makes him laugh every time. 'Simply the Best' makes him laugh more than 'Hard Rain is Going to Fall' because, after all, it's easier to laugh when money is pouring down on you than when someone is snatching it out of your wallet. And today, Uzi tells me, is a big day because he's planning to invest a packet in NASDAQ options. Those options are called QQQQ, but Uzi thinks it's funnier to call them 'cuckoo'. If the NASDAQ goes up, so do they. And since the NASDAQ, according to Uzi, is going to fly through the ceiling any minute, all we have to do is grab the cuckoo by the tail and fly with it to the sky.

It takes Uzi twenty minutes to explain this, and when he's finished, he checks his mobile phone display again. When he began his explanation, the cuckoo was 1.3, and now it's already 1.55. 'We're pathetic,' Uzi laments as he chews his almond croissant, spraying crumbs all over the place. 'Do you realise that in just this last half-hour, we could have made more than 10 per cent on our money?'

'Why do you keep saying "we"?' I ask. 'And what money are you talking about? Do you think I have money to put into this thing?'

'You don't have to put in a lot,' Uzi says. 'If we'd put in five thousand, we'd be five hundred ahead. But we didn't. You know what? Forget it, why am I making you a part of this? I didn't. And that's even though, deep down, I knew for an absolute fact – the way a baby knows that his mother will always love him – that NASDAQ would break 1.5.'

'There are mothers who abandon their babies,' I say.

'Maybe,' Uzi mumbles, 'but not the cuckoo's mother. I'm telling you, I should have put all my money on it, but I decided to wait. And you know why? Because I'm a loser.'

'You're not . . .' I try, but Uzi's too far into it to stop. 'Look at me, I'm thirty-five and I don't even have a million.'

'But just a week ago you told me you invested more than a million in the market,' I say.

'Shekels,' Uzi snorts contemptuously, 'what's a million shekels? I'm talking dollars here.' Uzi swallows the last piece of croissant sadly and washes it down with a swig of Diet Coke. 'Look around,' he says. 'Pimple-faced teenagers who served me coffee in styrofoam cups at start-ups created by me are driving BMWs while I drive a Peugeot 205 like some dental hygienist.'

'Stop moaning,' I tell him. 'Believe me, a lot of people would kill to swap places with you.'

'A lot of people?' Uzi laughs to himself, half maliciously. 'A lot of which people? A lot of the jobless in Sderot? A lot of lepers in India? What's got into you, Dedi? Have you turned Amish on me now? Looks to me like that divorce fucked you up completely.'

Uzi and I have known each other since we were about three. A lot of time has passed since then, but not a lot has changed. Uzi says that even then I felt sorry for myself all the time.

When we were in our last year at school, I fanta-
sised about having a girlfriend while Uzi was
already trying to make a killing. He started a
summer camp for kids. His business plan was
simple: the money he got from the parents he
split fifty–fifty with the kids, and in return, the
kids didn't tell on him for not organising any
activities except for tossing a ratty football on the
grass for them to kick around and letting them
drink from the water fountain once every two
hours. Today Uzi has his own flat, a wife who
was once a secretary in some dot com company
he worked for, and a chubby little daughter who
looks just like him. 'If we get divorced now,' Uzi
says, 'she gets half. Of everything. And it's all
because I was a pussy before the wedding and
didn't make her sign a pre-nup.'

I've already paid for breakfast and now we're
waiting for the change. 'You, on the other hand,'
Uzi continues, 'came out of your divorce like a
champ. She didn't take a shekel.'

'That's because there was nothing to take.' I try
to put the compliment into perspective.

'For the time being,' Uzi pats me on the back,
'for the time being. And now that the whole

117

business between the two of you is signed and sealed, this is the perfect time to strike and be the only winner, like in the one-winner sweepstakes, without partners.'

'Without partners,' I repeat automatically and swallow the last, sweetest drops of my coffee.

'Without partners,' Uzi repeats, 'just me and you. I have a feeling that the cuckoo is going to drop a bit again, not really low, to maybe 1.35, and then we buy. We buy the socks off it.' The waitress doesn't come back with the change. The owner walks over instead. 'Excuse me,' he says, 'I'm very sorry to bother you, but the hundred-shekel note you gave the waitress is counterfeit. Look.' He holds the note up to the light. 'It's not real.' I take the note and look at the watermark. Instead of a drawing of former President ben Zvi, a scribbled smiley face looks out at me.

'Counterfeit?' Uzi snatches the note out of my hand. 'Let me see,' he says, and tosses the owner a different note, which he examines against the light too. Meanwhile, I apologise. 'I took a taxi here and paid the driver with a two-hundred-shekel note,' I tell the owner. 'He must have palmed the fake note off on me as change.'

'This note, it's so cool,' Uzi says. 'Will you sell it to me? For a hundred?'

'What are you so excited about?' I ask Uzi. 'It's counterfeit.'

'That's why, you idiot,' Uzi says and takes a wad of notes out of his wallet. 'Non-counterfeits I already have. But counterfeit is classy. I'll dump it on anyone who gives me crap service.'

'OK,' I say, 'have it. A counterfeit hundred as a gift from me.'

Now we're in Uzi's car. We just got in. I don't know why I told him that I cry at night. Uzi is not exactly the person to share stuff like that with. 'And it's not because of her,' I stress, 'I don't want her to come back.'

'Yeah, I know,' Uzi mumbles, 'I know her.' His mobile tells him he's simply the best, but he doesn't even glance at the screen to see how much the stock has gone up, he just moves his face right up to mine and stares at me from an inch away like a doctor examining a patient. 'You know what you need, and right now?' he says. 'An Ethiopian sand-wich at 56 Matalon Street.'

'We've just eaten,' I protest.

'A sandwich isn't food,' Uzi says, fiddling with

the steering-wheel lock, 'a sandwich is one Ethiopian chick under you and another one on top of you, pressing her tits into your back. I have to tell you that when I first heard about it, it didn't turn me on either, but it really is amazing.'

'What's 56 Matalon Street?' I ask. 'A brothel?'

'Let's not change the subject,' Uzi says, turning on the ignition, 'we're talking about you now. You haven't fucked even once since you and Ofra split up, have you?'

I nod and say, 'And I don't feel like it either.'

'In life,' Uzi releases the handbrake, 'you don't always do what you feel like.'

'If you're trying to tell me that I cry because I'm not fucking, then you're wrong,' I object.

'I'm not saying that.' Uzi drums the wheel with his fingers. 'I'm saying that you cry because your life is empty. Because it has no meaning. And when you're empty inside . . .' he touches himself on the chest slightly to the right of his heart, 'if there's meaning around you, you put some of it inside yourself, and if there isn't, you shove in a plug. Just for the time being, till the manufacturer sends along the meaning. And in cases like that, an Ethiopian sandwich is a great plug.'

'Take me home,' I say. 'My life is pathetic enough without going to whores.' But Uzi isn't with me any more. His phone is ringing again with an unfamiliar, boring ringtone programmed for incoming calls. It's someone from the bank. Uzi tells him to buy $20,000 of the QQQQ, which has gone down again. 'Ten thousand for me and another ten thousand for a friend.'

I shake my head at him, but Uzi ignores me. And when he hangs up he says, 'Get used to it, Dedi, you and me, we're gonna grab the cuckoo by the tail.'

Through the thin wall I can hear Uzi's phone sing to him that he's simply the best and a woman roaring with laughter. There were no Ethiopians at 56 Matalon Street today, so Uzi went into a room with a big-boobed girl who said in English that she was Czech, and I have a bottle blonde, probably Russian. On the other side of the wall, Uzi is laughing out loud now too – I guess a Czech open sandwich isn't a bad plug either. The blonde's name is Maria and she asks me if I want her to help me get undressed. I tell her that won't be necessary, that I'm only there because of my crazy friend and that as far as I'm concerned, we can just sit there together till Uzi finishes and then leave, without fucking. 'No fuck?' Maria tries to understand. 'Suck?' On the other side of the wall, Uzi's mobile keeps telling him he's simply the best. Something good is happening in there. Maria unbuttons my trousers and I tell myself that if I ask her to stop, she'll be insulted. I know that isn't true, but I make an effort to believe it. Maybe Uzi is right and all I need now is a plug. While she's doing it, I try to invent a life for her, a happy one that brought her to prostitution out of choice. I once saw a film like that, about a cheerful, big-hearted French whore. Maybe Maria's that way too, only Russian. When I look down, all I can see is her hair. Every once in a while she raises her head and asks, 'Is good?' and I nod in embarrassment. Soon it'll be over.

During the half-hour we spend at 56 Matalon Street, the cuckoo flies right through the ceiling. By the time we're back on the sun-baked street, it has already reached 1.75, which, according to Uzi, gives us a hundred per cent on our money. And so the cuckoo continues to slice through the blue sky like a kite, with us right behind it, clutching its tail tightly, trying not to fall.

Pick a Colour

A black man moved into a white neighbourhood. He had a black house with a black porch where he used to sit every morning and drink his black coffee, until one black night, his white neighbours came into his house and beat the shit out of him. He lay there curled up like an umbrella handle in a pool of black blood and they kept on beating him, until one of them started yelling that they should stop because if he died on them they might end up in prison.

The black man didn't die on them. An ambulance came and took him far, far away to an enchanted hospital on the top of an inactive volcano. The hospital was white. Its gates were white, the walls of its rooms were white, and so was the bedding. The black man began to recover. Recover and fall in love. Fall in love with a white nurse in a white uniform who took care of him with great devotion and kindness. She loved him too. And like him, that love of theirs grew stronger with every passing day, grew stronger and learned to get out of bed and crawl. Like a small child. Like a baby. Like a black man who had been badly beaten.

They got married in a yellow church. A yellow priest married them. His yellow parents had come to that country on a yellow ship. They had been beaten up by their white neighbours too. But he didn't get into all that with the black man. He barely knew him, and anyway, he didn't want to go there, what with the ceremony and everything. He planned to say that God loves them and wishes them all the best. The yellow man didn't know that for sure. He'd tried lots of times to convince himself that he did. That he knows that God loves everyone and wishes us all only the best. But that day, when he married that battered black man, not even thirty and already covered with scars and sitting in a wheelchair, it was harder for him to believe. 'God loves you both,' he finally said anyway. 'God loves you and wishes you all the best,' he said and was ashamed.

The black man and the white woman lived together happily, until one day, when the woman was walking home from the supermarket, a brown man with a brown knife who was waiting for her in the stairwell told her to give him everything she had. When the black man came home, he found her dead. He didn't understand why the brown man had stabbed her, because he could have just taken her money and run. The funeral service took place in the yellow priest's yellow church, and when the black man saw the yellow priest, he grabbed him by his yellow robe and said, 'But you told us. You told us that God loves us. If He loves us, why did He do such a terrible thing to us?' The yellow priest had a ready-made answer. An answer they'd taught him in priest school; something about God working in mysterious ways and that now that the woman was dead, she was surely closer to Him. But instead of using that answer, the priest began cursing. He cursed God viciously. Insulting and hurtful curses the likes of which had never been heard in the world before. Curses so insulting and hurtful that even God was offended.

God entered the yellow church on the disabled ramp. He was in a wheelchair too; he had once lost a woman too. He was silvery. Not the cheap, glittery silver of a banker's BMW, but a muted, matt silver. Once, as He was gliding among the silvery stars with his silvery beloved, a gang of golden gods attacked them. When they were children, God had once beaten one of them up, a short, skinny golden god who had now grown up and returned with his friends. The golden gods beat Him with golden clubs of sunlight and didn't stop until they'd broken every bone in His divine body. It took Him years to recuperate. His beloved never did. She remained a vegetable. She could see and hear everything, but she couldn't say a word. The silvery God decided to create a species in His own image so she could watch it to pass the time. That species really did resemble Him: battered and victimised like Him. And His silvery beloved stared wide-eyed at the members of that species for hours, stared and didn't even shed a tear.

'What do you think,' the silvery God asked the yellow priest in frustration, 'that I created all of you like this because it's what I wanted? Because I'm some kind of pervert or sadist who enjoys all this suffering? I created you like this because this is what I know. It's the best I can do.'

The yellow priest fell to his knees and begged His forgiveness. If a stronger God had come to his church, he probably would have carried on cursing Him, even if he had to go to hell for it. But seeing the silvery, disabled God made him feel regret and sorrow, and he really did want His forgiveness. The black man didn't fall to his knees. With the bottom half of his body paralysed, he couldn't do things like that any more. He just sat in his wheelchair and pictured a silvery goddess somewhere in the heavens looking down at him with gaping eyes. That imbued him with a sense of purpose, of hope, even. He couldn't explain to himself exactly why, but the thought that he was suffering just like a god made him feel blessed.

Black and Blue

In A & E they said the bone was fractured and the muscle was nearly torn in two places. Some people, the doctor said, can walk away from a fifty-mile-an-hour head-on collision without a scratch. Once there was this man who arrived in A & E, a fat guy who'd fallen out of his third-floor flat onto the pavement, and all he had was a black-and-blue mark on his backside. It's all a matter of luck. Which she, apparently, didn't have much of. One wrong move on her way down the stairs, an ankle that turned the wrong way – and here she was, in hospital, with a cast.

A man who looked like an Arab wrapped the wet bandages around her foot. He told her he was just an intern and that, if she wanted, she could wait for the doctor to do it, but it would take at least another hour, because they had a backlog.

When he'd finished with the cast, he told her that because it was summer, it would itch all the time. He didn't give her any tips on what to do about this, just the fact. A few minutes later, it really did begin to itch.

If it hadn't been for the cast, she wouldn't have been home when David phoned. If it hadn't been for the cast, she would have been at work. He told her he was in Tel Aviv, he'd come to Israel just for a week, to attend some conference, something to do with the Jewish Agency. He said he was wasting away in those lectures and he wanted to see her, and she said OK. If it hadn't been for the cast, she'd have made some excuse and talked her way out of it, but she was bored. If he came, she thought, there would be the excitement leading up to it. She'd stand in front of the mirror and choose a top and do her eyebrows. Then, when he came, probably nothing would happen, but at least she'd have enjoyed the build-up. Anyway, what did she have to lose? With anyone else, she'd be worrying about being let down, but with David there was nothing left to worry about. The man had already let her down the last time they met, going on about how much he loved her and, after they messed around a bit and she gave him a handjob, falling asleep on his hotel bed. He hadn't called the next day, nor the day after that. And two days later, she'd stopped expecting him to. She knew he'd gone back to Cleveland, or Portland, or whatever his home town in America was called. And it hurt. It hurt like when someone sees you in the street and pretends they don't recognise you. If she were to meet him in the street in Cleveland or Portland, or wherever, and he'd been there with his girlfriend, she just knew that's what would have happened.

Back then, he told her about his girlfriend. And that they were going to get married. She couldn't claim he'd kept it from her. But there was something in the way he said it that made her feel like it had been true until the moment he met her and that now his life was taking a whole new direction, one that included her. But she must have got it wrong, or he must have given her the wrong impression. It all depends on how you look at it. And on the mood she was in when she pictured the two of them at the hotel. Sometimes she'd tell herself, come off it, you moron. He's American, what did you expect? You think he'd dump his whole life over there – the job at the JCC that he tried to tell you about? That he'd come here to work as a barman or a delivery boy just to be with you? But other times, she'd get angry. Why did he have to use that word 'love'? He could have just told her he was attracted to her or that he was horny, drunk and far from home. Chances were she'd have given him a handjob anyway, but without hanging around at home for two days afterwards waiting for the phone to ring. She didn't have a mobile phone back then, so she just sat around and waited. It was summer then too, and her flat wasn't air-conditioned. The air in the room wasn't moving, and all day long she tried to read a book – *Underworld* by Don DeLillo – but by the end of the day she was still stuck at Chapter 1. She couldn't remember a thing she'd read. Something about a baseball game. She never went back to it after that, and David never called. But now, almost a year later, suddenly he did, and when he asked if he could come over, she said OK, mainly because she didn't want him to notice that a part of her had been hurt. She didn't want him to think he mattered so much that she wouldn't want to see him again.

He brought a bottle of wine and a pizza. Half olive, half anchovy. He didn't even phone to ask her what she wanted or if she was hungry at all. But the pizza was really good. The wine was white and warm, but they didn't have the patience to wait for it to chill, so they drank it with ice cubes. 'A hundred-dollar bottle,' he said, laughing, 'and here we are, drinking it like Diet Coke.' He must have wanted her to know he'd spent a lot of money on the wine. Since that night, he said, I've been feeling really awful about what happened. I felt like shit. I should have phoned you the next morning to explain. In fact, I should have made sure it never happened in the first place. I'm sorry. And she patted his cheek, not seductively, but more like a mother comforting her son who's just owned up to cheating in an exam, and telling him it's not so terrible. Yes, she had thought about him. She'd wondered why he hadn't called. But anyway, he shouldn't feel bad about it. He'd told her from the start that he had a girlfriend and that was that.

They'd got married in the meantime, David told her. When he got back from Israel, Karen – that was her name – told him she was pregnant and they'd had to decide whether to have an abortion or stay together. When Karen talked to him about it – it was as soon as he got off the plane and he'd still had her scent in his hair. He hadn't showered since that night they were in bed together, so that the scent would linger. They'd had to decide whether to have an abortion or to stay together, Karen said. And he hadn't wanted to stay together. Because of her, because of that night. But he didn't want Karen to have an abortion either. It was hard for him to explain. He wasn't religious or anything. But the thought of an abortion seemed so irreversible and made him very uneasy. So he proposed. A baby is also irreversible, she told him now, as if it was a joke, and he cringed and said he knew that. And in the same breath, he added that it was a baby girl, and that it was the most wonderful thing that had ever happened to him. Even if he and Karen got divorced, he said, which he didn't think would happen, because they were doing OK on the whole, but even if it did happen, he was glad that Karen hadn't had an abortion. Their little girl was so incredibly adorable. On Friday she'd be five months old exactly, and this was the first time he'd been away since she was born. He'd almost decided not to come to this conference either. He must have changed his mind five times at least, but in the end he took the flight. Mainly to see her. To tell her he was sorry.

'I came here to ask you to forgive me,' he said again. She wanted to tell him he was making too much of it. A mountain out of a molehill. But after another drawn-out silence, she said she forgave him. She'd never been in his situation, but she understood him completely. And she was just a bit sorry that he'd never called. To say goodbye before he took off, that's all. 'If I'd called,' he said, 'I would have come back. And if I'd come back, I would have fallen in love with you. I was scared.' And if she'd wanted to make him feel bad, she could have mentioned that even back then, on that first night, he'd said he loved her, but instead, she just stroked his large hand as it rested on the table, and later they went into the living room together and watched an episode of *Lost* and finished off the wine. Three years ago, when Giora got her pregnant, she hadn't even asked him if he wanted her to have an abortion or wanted them to stay together. She just went ahead and had the abortion without telling him. Two months later, they split up. This David must have loved Karen a little more than she'd loved Giora. Or at least hated her less. She knew that this night could end wherever she wanted it to, and it made her feel strong. If she drew things out a bit till it got late and said she was tired, he would leave without trying anything. If she looked at him and smiled – he'd kiss her. She could tell. But what did she really want? For him to go back to his hotel room horny and masturbate and think about her, about how things had worked out OK? Or for him to spend the night with her and feel like shit the next day? She kept changing her mind. Forget about him, she told herself, forget about him and about how he'll feel. Think about yourself. What do you want?

Because of the cast, going to the loo was a whole performance now. She had to hop on one leg and keep her balance. David wouldn't let her do this. He picked her up in his arms, like a fireman saving her from a burning building or a groom carrying her over the threshold on their wedding night. He waited behind the door as she peed, and then carried her back into the living room. By the time they were settled again, the episode was over. David told her the ending. He'd seen it already. In America, they screen it a week earlier. He hadn't told her before that he'd already seen it, because he didn't mind watching it again, with her. He wasn't much of a TV buff anyway. The first time, he'd only watched it because Karen was addicted to the series. It's hot in your flat, he said. Stifling hot. She told him she knew. The owner had lowered the rent for her and her flatmate by two hundred shekels because there was no air conditioner. Since she'd broken her leg, she was stuck here, she said. At the hospital, they'd given her a pair of crutches, but who has the strength to walk down four flights of stairs on crutches? And before she realised what was happening, he lifted her up, piggyback, and they walked down the four flights. Just like that.

He carried her that way to Meyer Park, where they sat on a bench and smoked a cigarette. It was hot and humid there too, but at least there was a breeze to dry off the perspiration. Having you forgive me was really important to me, he said. Extremely important. I can't even explain why. It's not that I never behaved like shit before with girls I dated, but with you . . . he started crying. It took her a moment to realise this was what he was doing. At first she thought he was coughing or choking or something, but he was simply crying. Stop it, you idiot, she told him, half smiling. People are staring. They'll think I threw you out, I broke your heart. I am an idiot, David told her, I really am. I could have . . . you've never been to Cleveland, have you? Talk about Cleveland and talk about Tel Aviv. She could tell he wanted to say, Talk about Karen and talk about you, and she was glad he didn't say it.

They walked back up the four flights of stairs very slowly. He couldn't carry her any more, so she just leaned on him and hobbled up, step after step. By the time they reached the door, they were both sweating, and inside her cast, the maddening itch was starting up again. Do you want me to go? he asked, and she shook her head, but what she said was that she thought it would be a good idea. Afterwards, in bed, facing the fan, she tried to make sense of the whole story. An American guy and an Israeli girl meet by sheer chance. One nice evening. A little spit on her left palm sliding up and down David's cock. And two people, on two sides of the world, end up carrying around

all these not-very-important details for almost a
year. Some people fall out of the third floor of
a building and end up with nothing more than a
black-and-blue mark on their backside. While
others take one wrong step on their way down the
stairs and end up with a cast. She and David
were of the second kind.

What Do We Have in Our Pockets?

A cigarette lighter, a cough sweet, a postage stamp, a slightly bent cigarette, a toothpick, a handkerchief, a pen, two five-shekel coins. That's only a fraction of what I have in my pockets. So is it any wonder they bulge? Lots of people mention it. They say, 'What the fuck do you have in your pockets?' Most of the time I don't answer, I just smile, sometimes I even give a short, polite laugh. As if someone has told me a joke. If they were to persist and ask me again, I'd probably show them everything I have, I might even explain why I need all that stuff on me, always. But they don't. What the fuck, a smile, a short laugh, an awkward silence, and we're on to the next subject.

The fact is that everything I have in my pockets

is carefully chosen so I'll always be prepared. Everything is there so I can be at an advantage at the moment of truth. Actually, that's not accurate. Everything's there so I won't be at a disadvantage at the moment of truth. Because what kind of advantage can a wooden toothpick or a postage stamp really give you? But if, for example, a beautiful girl – you know what, not even beautiful, just charming, an ordinary-looking girl with an entrancing smile that takes your breath away – asks you for a stamp, or doesn't even ask, just stands there on the street next to a red postbox on a rainy night with a stampless envelope in her hand and wonders if you happen to know where there's an open post office at that hour, and then gives a little cough because she's cold, but also desperate, since deep in her heart, she knows that there's no open post office in the area, definitely not at that hour, and at that moment, that moment of truth, she won't say, 'What the fuck do you have in your pockets?' but she'll be so grateful for the stamp, maybe not even grateful, she'll just smile that entrancing smile of hers, an entrancing smile for a postage stamp – I'd go for a deal like that any time, even if the price of stamps soars and the price of smiles plummets.

After the smile, she'll say thank you and cough again, because of the cold, but also because she's a bit embarrassed. And I'll offer her a cough sweet. 'What else do you have in your pockets?' she'll ask, but gently, without the 'fuck' and without the negativity, and I'll answer without hesitation: everything you'll ever need, my love. Everything you'll ever need.

So now you know. That's what I have in my pockets. A chance not to screw up. A slight chance. Not big, not even probable. I know that, I'm not stupid. A tiny chance, let's say, that when happiness comes along, I can say 'Yes' to it, and not 'Sorry, I don't have a cigarette/toothpick/coin for the drinks machine'. That's what I have there, full and bulging, a tiny chance of saying yes and not being sorry.

Bad Karma

'**Fifteen** shekels a month can guarantee your daughter one hundred thousand in the event of your death, God forbid. Do you know what a difference one hundred thousand can make to a young orphan? It's exactly the difference between life in a white-collar profession and life as a receptionist in a dentist's office.'

Since the accident, Oshri had been selling policies like hot cakes. It wasn't clear whether this had to do with his slight limp or with the paralysis in his right arm, but people who'd sit through an appointment with him would lap it all up, and buy everything he had to offer: life insurance, loss of earning power, complementary health insurance, you name it. At first Oshri kept recycling the one about the Yemenite who was run over by an ice-cream van the very day he bought his policy, on his way to pick up his daughter from nursery, or the one about the man from the suburbs who'd laughed when Oshri had offered him health insurance and one month later called in tears, having just received a diagnosis of pancreatic cancer. But very soon he realised that his own personal story did the trick better than any of the others. There he was, Oshri Sivan, insurance salesman, in the middle of a meeting with a potential client at a cafe near the Downtown Shopping Arcade, when all of a sudden, right in the middle of their conversation, a young man who'd decided to end his life jumps out of an eleventh-floor window in the building next to them, and wham! falls right on Oshri's head. The fall kills the young man, and Oshri, who has just finished telling his Yemenite-and-ice-cream-van story to another reluctant client, loses consciousness on the spot. He doesn't come to when they splash water over his face, or in the ambulance, or in A & E, and not even in the ICU. He's in a coma. The doctors say it's touch and go. His wife sits by his bedside and cries and cries, and so does his little girl. Nothing changes for six weeks, until all of a sudden a miracle occurs: Oshri comes out of

143

his coma, as if nothing had happened. He simply opens his eyes and gets up. And along with this miracle comes a bitter truth: our Oshri didn't practise what he preached, and since he'd never had any insurance whatsoever himself, he couldn't keep up with his mortgage and had to sell his flat and move into a rented place. 'Look at me,' Oshri would end his sad story, with a lame attempt to move his right arm. 'Look at me, sitting here with you in this cafe, spitting blood to sell you a policy. If only I'd put aside thirty shekels a month. Thirty shekels, which is nothing really, barely a matinee ticket – without the popcorn – I'd be lying back like a king, with two hundred grand in my account. Me, I had my chance and I blew it, but you – aren't you going to learn from my mistake, Motti? Sign on the dotted line and get it over with. Who knows what could land on your head five minutes from now.' And this Motti or Yigal or Mickey sitting opposite him would stare for a minute and then take the pen he held out with his good arm and sign. Every single one of them. No ifs, ands or buts. And Oshri would wink goodbye, because when your right arm is paralysed there's no shaking hands, and on his way out he'd be sure to add something about how they'd made the right move. And so, without much effort, Oshri Sivan's battered bank account quickly began to recover, and within three months he and his wife had bought a new flat with a much smaller mortgage than the one they'd had before. And with all the physiotherapy he got at the clinic, even his arm started to get better, though when clients held out their hand to him, he'd still pretend he couldn't move it at all.

'**There's** blue and yellow and white and a soft sweet taste in my mouth. There's something hovering high above me. Something good, and I'm heading towards it. Heading towards it.'

At night he went on dreaming about it – not about the accident. About the coma. It was strange, but even though a long time had passed since then, he could still remember, down to the last detail, everything he'd felt during those six weeks. He remembered the colours and the taste and the fresh air cooling his face. He remembered the absence of memory, the sense of existing without a name and without a history, in the present. Six whole weeks of present. During which the only thing he felt within him that wasn't the present was this little hint of a future, in the form of an unaccountable optimism attached to a strange sense of beingness. He didn't know what his own name was during those six weeks, or that he was married or that he had a little girl. He didn't know he'd had an accident or that he was in hospital now, fighting for his life. He didn't know anything except that he was alive. And this fact alone filled him with enormous happiness. All in all, the experience of thinking and feeling within that nothingness was more intense than anything that had ever happened to him before, as if all the background noises had disappeared and the only sound left was true and pure and beautiful to the point of tears. He didn't discuss it with his wife or with anyone else. You're not supposed to get that much joy out of being close to death. You're not supposed to get a thrill from your coma while your wife and daughter are crying their hearts out at your bedside. So when they asked whether he remembered anything about it, he said he didn't, he didn't remember a thing. When he woke up, his wife asked if, when he'd been in the coma, he'd been able to hear her and Meital, their daughter, talking to him, and he told

her that even if he couldn't remember hearing
them he was sure it had helped him. It had given
him strength, on the unconscious level, and a desire
to live. That was what he told her but it wasn't
true because when he was in a coma he really did
hear voices on the outside sometimes. Strange,
sharp, yet at the same time unclear, like sounds
you hear when you're under water. And he didn't
like it at all. Those voices sounded menacing to
him, they hinted at something beyond the pleasant,
colourful now in which he was living.

'May you never know sorrow again.'

Oshri couldn't make it during the shiva week to
pay a condolence call on the family of the man
who'd fallen on his head. He couldn't make it to
the unveiling of the headstone either. But when the
first anniversary came round, he did go, with flowers
and everything. At the cemetery there were only
the man's parents and his sister and some fat school
friend. They didn't know who he was. The mother
thought he was her son's boss, whose name was
Oshri too. The sister and the fat man thought he
was a friend of the parents. But after everyone had

finished placing little stones on the grave and the mother started asking around, he explained that he was the one that Nattie, that was the man's name, had landed on when he jumped out the window. As soon as the mother heard this, she started saying how sorry she was, and couldn't stop crying. The father tried to calm her down, and kept giving Oshri suspicious looks. After five minutes of her hysterical sobbing, the father told Oshri stiffly how sorry he was for everything that had happened to him and that he was sure that Nattie too, if he were still alive, would be sorry, but that now it would be better for everyone if Oshri left. Oshri agreed at once and quickly added that he was almost fine by now and that at the end of the day it hadn't been so terrible – certainly not when you compared it to what Nattie's parents had been through. The father cut him short in mid-sentence: 'Are you planning to sue us? Because if you are, you're wasting your time. Ziva and I haven't got a penny to our names, you hear me? Not a penny.' The words only made the mother cry harder, and Oshri mumbled something that was supposed to reassure them, about how he had no hard feelings against anyone, and after that, he left. As he was putting the cardboard yarmulke back in the wooden box at the entrance to the cemetery, Nattie's sister caught up with him and apologised for her father. She didn't exactly apologise, actually, just said that he was an idiot and that Nattie had always hated him. His father, it turned out, had always been sure everyone was out to get him and in the end that was what really happened, when his partner ran off with his money. 'If Nattie could see how things here turned out, he'd be laughing hysterically,' the sister said and introduced herself by name. Her name was Maayan. Out of habit, Oshri didn't take the hand she held out to him. After a year of pretending with clients that his arm was utterly paralysed, it had got to the point where even when he was alone at home he sometimes forgot he could use it. When Maayan saw that he wasn't taking her outstretched hand, she shifted the handshake ever so naturally and touched him on the shoulder – which, it turned out, made both of them a little uneasy. 'It's strange having you here,' she said after they had both been silent for a moment. 'What is Nattie to you? You didn't even know him, after all.' 'That's a shame,' Oshri said, not sure how to respond. 'That I didn't know him, I mean. He sounds like somebody who was definitely worth knowing.' Oshri wanted to tell her that his coming there wasn't strange at all. That he and her brother had some unfinished business between them. There had been so many people at the cafe that day, and of all the people there, he was the one that Nattie had dropped on top of. And that was why he'd come today, to try and understand why. But even before he had a chance to say it, he realised it would sound stupid, so he asked her instead why Nattie had killed himself – so young and everything. Maayan shrugged. He wasn't the first person to ask her that. Before they went their separate ways, he gave her his business card and said that if she needed any help, no matter what it was, she should call. And she smiled and thanked him but said she was someone who managed very well on her own. After taking another look at the card, she said: 'You're an insurance salesman? That's really strange. Nattie always hated insurance, said it was bad karma. That taking out a policy was like the opposite of believing things would go well.' Oshri got defensive. Lots of young people think that way, he said, but once you have children you look at things differently. And even if you want to believe things will go well, you can never be too careful.

'Still, if you need anything,' he told her before she left, 'do call. I promise not to try to sell you insurance.' And she smiled and nodded. They both knew she wouldn't be calling.

While Oshri was on his way home from the cemetery, his wife phoned. She wanted him to pick up Meital from the class she had after school. Oshri agreed straightaway, and when she asked him where he was, he lied and said he'd had an appointment with a client in Ramat Hasharon. He couldn't explain to himself why he'd lied. It wasn't because of the touch he could still feel on his shoulder, and it wasn't because he'd gone to the memorial service for no good reason. If anything, it was because he was afraid she'd get a sense of how grateful he was to that man, Nattie, who must have been just as clever, as successful and as loved as Oshri was, and had still decided to put an end to it all and jump out the window. When he picked up Meital, she proudly showed him a model aeroplane she'd built and he admired it and asked her when she was planning to fly it in the sky. 'Never,' Meital said, and gave him a derisive look. 'It's just a model.' And Oshri nodded, embarrassed, and said she was such a clever little girl.

'Pleasant dreams'

Ever since the accident, he and his wife made love a lot less often. They never talked about it, but he had the feeling she thought it was OK too. As if after the accident and everything she was just so glad to have him back that she wasn't planning to keep score. Whenever they did make love it was nice, just as nice as it had been before, except that now his life had taken on another perspective, one that had to do with that world, a world you can only reach when something falls on you from the top floor, a perspective that seemed to have dwarfed everything else. Not just the sex, but his love for her too, and his love for his daughter, everything.

When he was awake he couldn't remember exactly what it had felt like to be in the world of the coma, and if he tried to describe it to someone, he couldn't. He only tried once, with this blind woman that he'd been trying to sell life insurance to. He wasn't sure why he'd expected her, of all people, to understand, but after three sentences he realised he was only scaring her, so he stopped. In his dreams, though, he really could go back there. And ever since that day in the cemetery, his coma dreams recurred more often. He felt himself becoming addicted to them. So much so that in the evenings, long before he got into bed, he would begin to tremble in anticipation, like someone who after many years in exile was getting on the flight that would take him home. It's funny, but sometimes he was so excited that he couldn't even fall asleep. And then he'd find himself lying in bed, frozen, next to his sleeping wife, trying to lull himself to sleep in all sorts of ways. One of them was masturbation. And ever since that memorial service, whenever he masturbated, he'd think of Maayan, of how she'd touched him on his shoulder. It wasn't because she was beautiful. And it wasn't that she wasn't beautiful, though her beauty was the fragile kind that comes with youth, the kind whose expiry date was coming up very, very soon. As it happened, his wife had once had that same kind of beauty, many years ago, when they first met. But that wasn't the reason he would think of Maayan. It was because of the connection between her and the man who had helped him reach that world of colours and quiet, and when he'd masturbate over Maayan, it was as if he was masturbating over a world that suddenly, thanks to her, had taken on a woman's shape.

Meanwhile, he was churning out policies at a dizzying pace. Without even meaning to, he was getting better and better at it. Now, when he tried to sell them, he'd often find himself in tears. It wasn't a manipulation. It was real crying that came out of nowhere. And it would shorten the meetings. Oshri would cry and then he'd apologise, and right away the clients would say it was OK and sign. It made him feel a bit like a swindler, the crying, though it was as genuine as could be.

'Congestion on the coastal road'

One weekend when they were returning with their daughter from a visit to his wife's parents on a kibbutz, they passed a two-car collision. The drivers ahead of them slowed down to rubberneck, and his wife said it was disgusting, and that only in Israel did people behave that way. Their daughter, who'd been asleep in the back, woke up because of the ambulance sirens. She put her face up to the window and looked out at a man covered in blood, unconscious, being carried away on a stretcher. She asked them where they were taking him and Oshri told her they were taking him to a good place. A place filled with colours and tastes and smells that you couldn't even imagine. He told her about that place, about how your body becomes weightless there, and how even though you don't want anything, everything there comes true. How there's no fear there, so that even if something is going to hurt, when it happens it turns into just another kind of feeling, a feeling that you're grateful to be able to have. He went on and on until he noticed the angry look on his wife's face. On the radio they reported heavy traffic on the motorway, and when he looked in the rear-view mirror again he could see Meital smiling and waving bye-bye at the man on the stretcher.

Ari

When she comes, my girlfriend screams out, 'Ari.' Not just once, a lot. 'Ari-Ari-Ari-Ari!' And that's just fine, as I'm an Ari born and bred. Still, sometimes I kind of want her to shout something else, it wouldn't matter what. 'My love.' 'Tear me in half.' 'Stop, I can't take any more.' Even a plain old 'Don't stop!' would do. It'd just be nice to hear something different once in a while, something specific to the occasion – an emotion a little more to the point.

My girlfriend is a law student at the local college. She wanted to go to one of the big universities but they didn't take her. Right now she's gearing up to specialise in contract law. There's really a thing like that, lawyers who only deal with contracts. They don't meet people, they don't appear in court, they just sit there all day looking at line after line printed on paper, as if that makes up a world.

She was there with me when I rented the flat. And within a minute she catches the owner trying to con us on some clause. In a million years I'd never have noticed, but she spotted it in a flash. My girlfriend, she's razor-sharp. And how she comes. My whole life, I've never seen anything like it. Her flying in every direction, body in full riot. It's like seeing someone electrocuted. She gets swallowed up by these waves of convulsions, involuntary ones, from deep inside. They rumble their way into her neck and tickle the soles of her feet. It's like her whole anatomy is trying to say thanks without knowing how.

Once I asked her what she used to shout when she came with other guys – back before me. She stared at me, surprised, and said that with all of them, when she came, she yelled 'Ari'. Always 'Ari'. And I couldn't let it go. I asked her what she used to say when she came with guys that didn't happen to be called Ari. She thought about it for a minute, and said that she'd never once fucked anyone who wasn't called Ari. Twenty-eight guys she'd already bedded, including me, and all of them – now that she was thinking back on it – were Aris, every last one. After she said it, she went silent. And then, really calmly, I told her, 'That's one crazy coincidence . . . or maybe that's your whole selection process, finding a new Ari.' 'Maybe,' she said, all thoughtful. 'Maybe.'

From that moment on, I became hyper-aware of all the Aris in my midst: there's the one at the falafel stand, and my accountant, and there's the pushy one at our coffee shop who's always asking me to put the sports section aside. I didn't make a big thing out of it, just made a mental note – Ari+Ari+Ari. Because deep down I knew, when all the torment is unleashed – if it's unleashed – it will spring from one of those guys.

It's strange to tell you so much about my girlfriend without even mentioning her name. As if it's of no importance at all. Except that it really isn't. If you woke me in the middle of the night, it's not her name that would come to mind. It would be that half-surprised look of hers one second before she starts to cry that would float through my head; or a vision of her arse; or that beautiful, childlike way she always says, 'I want to tell you something,' right before sharing a thought that moves her. My girl, she's fantastic. But sometimes I'm not so sure that this whole story will end well.

Our landlord, the one that tried to fleece us with the lease, he's also called Ari. He's basically nothing but a fifty-year-old prick, whose dead grandmother left him a whole building five blocks from the beach. Apart from collecting the rent from his tenants, the man hasn't done a stroke of work in his life. He's also got the kind of blue eyes you see on fighter pilots, and silver-grey hair that shines like the edge of a cloud. But this man's no pilot. When we signed the contract, he told me that he passed his whole military service pushing papers at Tzrifin, on some transport base. It'd been maybe a dozen years since his reserve unit even bothered to check where he was.

It was only by chance that I discovered he was fucking her. If she hadn't let me in on this whole story of the Aris, I wouldn't have been suspicious. When I caught them both in the flat, he was in the living room, fully dressed. He said he'd come round to check that we weren't 'destroying his assets'. As soon as he left, I pressed her and she came out and admitted it. But this was a confession with no guilt attached to it: when she spoke her tone was completely matter-of-fact, totally dry. Telling it to me the way a stranger would tell you the number 8 bus doesn't stop at Dizengoff. And as soon as she's finished, she says she has something to ask. What she wants to know is if we can all do it once, together. Him and me, both.

She's even willing to make a deal. If we do it just once, she won't ever see him again. Just once in her life she wants to feel a pair of Aris inside her together. He'll definitely agree, bored perv that he is. She's sure of it. And in the end I'll also give in, because I love her. I genuinely do.

And that's how I find myself in bed with my landlord. One second before he strips off he's still haranguing me about the shutters in the kitchen, that they don't close properly, that I need to oil some hinge. After a while, my girlfriend's body starts to shake up above me. I sense she's on her way. And I can tell that when she screams, somehow, everything will be all right. Because our name is truly Ari. Only, what we'll never know is if her scream is him or me.

Bitch

'Widower'. He loved the sound of that word so much, loved it, but at the same time, was ashamed that he loved it, but what can you do, love is an uncontrollable emotion. 'Bachelor' always sounded a bit egotistical to him, hedonistic, and 'divorced' – defeated, even more, wiped out. But 'widower'? 'Widower' sounds like someone who took responsibility, was committed, and if he was now on his own, you could only blame God or the forces of nature, depending on where you're coming from. He took out a cigarette and was about to light it when the anorexic girl sitting opposite him in the carriage started grumbling in French and pointing to the sign NON FUMEUR. Who would've believed that on the Marseilles–Paris train, they don't let a person light a Gauloise. Before he became a widower, every time he was about to light up, it was Bertha who broke into a monologue that began with his health and, somehow, always ended with her migraines, and now, when that too-skinny French girl told him off, he suddenly missed her.

'My wife,' he said to the French girl as he showed her that he was putting the cigarette back in the pack, 'also don't like me to smoke.'

'No English,' the French girl said.

'You,' he persisted, 'same age like my daughter. You should eat more. It is not healthy.'

'No English,' the French girl repeated, but her hunching shoulders gave her away, she understood every word.

'My daughter live in Marseilles,' he continued. 'She is married to a doctor, an eye doctor, you know,' and pointed at one of her green eyes, which were blinking in fear.

Even the coffee on the train was on a level three times higher than anything you could find in Haifa. Yessir, when it came to taste those damn French outclassed everyone. After a week in Marseilles, he couldn't button his trousers. Zahava had wanted him to stay longer. 'Where are you rushing off to?' she'd asked. 'Now that Mum's dead and you're retired, you're all alone.' 'Alone' and 'retired', there was something so open about those two words that when she said them, he could feel the wind on his face. After all, he'd never really liked working in the shop, and Bertha, well, he did have a soft spot for her, but, like the wooden wardrobe in their tiny bedroom, she took up so much space that there was no room left alongside her for anything else. The first thing he did after she died was call the man from the junkshop and get rid of that wardrobe. To the neighbours watching with interest as the huge wardrobe slid down from the third floor on belts, he explained that it reminded him too much of the tragedy. The tragedy. Now, without that wardrobe, the room had suddenly become spacious and lighter. After all those years, he'd forgotten a window was hidden behind it.

In the dining car, a woman of about seventy was sitting opposite him. She'd been beautiful once, and she did everything she could to remind people of that. But she did it subtly, with artful touches of lipstick and eyeliner. 'Ah . . . if you could only have seen me fifty years ago.' Next to her, on the shelf meant for food trays, sat a small poodle also dressed elegantly in an embroidered, powder-blue jumper. The poodle fixed huge, familiar eyes on him. 'Bertha?' he thought to himself, half terrified. The poodle gave a short bark in confirmation. The old woman flashed a pleasant smile at him that tried to say he had nothing to be afraid of. The poodle's eyes never left his. 'I know that wardrobe didn't fall on me by accident,' they said, 'I know you pushed it.' He took a short drag on his cigarette and shot a nervous smile back at the woman. 'And I know that you didn't want to kill me, that it was just a reflex. When I asked you to take down the winter clothes again, you just lost control.' His head seemed to nod on its own, another reflex, apparently. If he'd been someone else, less tough, there would already have been tears in his eyes. 'Are you happy now?' the poodle's eyes asked. 'So-so,' he looked back at it, 'It's hard alone. And you?' 'Not bad,' the poodle opened its mouth into almost a smile, 'My mistress takes care of me, she's a good woman. How's our daughter?' 'I've just been to her place. She looks wonderful and Gilbert finally agreed to try and have a baby.' 'I'm glad,' the poodle wagged its stumpy tail. 'But you, you have to take better care of yourself. You've got fat, and you smoke too much.' 'May I?' he asked the old woman without words, making petting motions in the air. The old woman nodded and smiled. He petted Bertha's whole body, then bent down and kissed her. 'I'm sorry,' he said in a broken, tearful voice, 'I'm sorry, Bertha, forgive me.' 'She love you,' the old woman said in broken English. 'Look, look how she lick your face. I never see her like that with a stranger.'

The Story, Victorious

This story is the best story in the book. More than that, this story is the best story in the world. And we weren't the ones to come to that conclusion. It was reached by a unanimous team of dozens of unaffiliated experts who – employing strict laboratory standards – measured it against a representative sampling taken from world litera-ture. This story is a unique Israeli innovation. And I bet you're asking yourselves, how is it that we (tiny little Israel) composed it, and not the Americans? What you should know is that the Americans are asking themselves the same thing. And more than a few of the bigwigs in American publishing stand to lose their jobs because they didn't have that answer at the ready while it still mattered.

Just as our army is the best army in the

world – same with this story. We're talking here
about an opening so innovative that it's protected
by registered patent. And where is this patent
registered? That's the thing, it's registered in the
story itself! This story's got no shtick to it, no trick
to it, no touchy-feely bits. It's forged from a single
block, an amalgam of deep insights and aluminium.
It won't rust, it won't bust, but it may wander. It's
super contemporary, and timelessly literary. Let
History be the judge! And by the way, according
to many fine folk, judgement's been passed – and
our story came up trumps.

'What's so special about this story?' people ask
out of innocence or ignorance (depending on
who's asking). 'What's it got that isn't in Chekhov
or Kafka or I-don't-know-who?' The answer to
that question is long and complicated. Longer than
the story itself, but less complex. Because there's
nothing more intricate than this story. Nevertheless,
we attempt to answer by example. In contrast to
works by Chekhov and Kafka, at the end of this
story, one lucky winner – randomly selected from
among all the correct readers – will receive a
brand-new Mazda Lantis with a metallic-grey
finish. And from among the incorrect readers, one

special someone will be selected to receive another car, cheaper, but no less impressive in its metallic greyness so that he or she shouldn't feel bad. Because this story isn't here to condescend. It's here so that you'll feel good. What's that saying printed on the place mats at the cafe near your house? ENJOYED YOURSELF – TELL YOUR FRIENDS! DIDN'T ENJOY YOURSELF – TELL US! Or, in this case – report it to the story. Because this story doesn't just tell, it also listens. Its ears, as they say, are attuned to every stirring of the public's heart. And when the public has had enough and calls for someone to put an end to it, this story won't drag its feet or grab hold of the edges of the altar. It will, simply, stop.

The Story, Victorious II

But if one day, out of nostalgia, you suddenly want the story back, it will always be happy to oblige.

A Good One

So real

The night before his flight to New York, Gershon's wife had a dream. 'It was so real,' she told him as he packed. 'In the dream, the kerbs were painted red and white and flats-for-sale ads were posted on the lamp posts, you know, the kind with those tabs you can pull off, just like in real life. There was even a man who scooped his dog's shit off the pavement with a piece of newspaper and threw it in a rubbish bin. And it was all so ordinary, so everyday.' Gershon was trying to cram more and more clothes and brochures into his small suitcase. His wife usually helped him pack, but this morning she was so engrossed in that so-real, so-detailed dream of hers that she didn't even offer to help. In the real world, the dream itself probably hadn't lasted more than ten seconds, but the way she managed to drag it out made Gershon so irritated that he was close to tears. In three hours' time he'd be on a plane to New York, on his way to meet the largest toy manufacturer in the world, and when we say 'largest in the world', that's not just another tired cliché, but a fact based on a large number of balance sheets and sales figures, and if Gershon played his cards right, that manufacturer might buy the Stop—Police board game Gershon had developed and turn it into no less than the twenty-first-century Monopoly. And while none of that is exactly a red-and-white kerb or a piece of dog shit being picked up with a wrinkled financial supplement, the idea that such monumental success might be on the horizon is the kind of thing you'd like to see your wife react to with a little more enthusiasm. '. . . And then my dad suddenly appears right in front of me with a pram and says to me, watch her. Just like that. Leaves the pram next to me and walks off like it's the most natural thing in the world,' his wife continued, as Gershon tried unsuccessfully to zip up his suitcase. 'And the baby girl in the pram looked so sad and alone, like an old woman, that I just wanted to take her in my arms and hug her. And it was all so real that when I woke up it took me a minute to work out how I'd gone from the middle of the street to our bedroom. You know that feeling?'

Restless

The albino sitting next to him tried to start a conversation. Gershon answered politely but didn't open up. He'd flown enough times to know the dynamic. There are some people who are just open and pleasant, and there are others who try to develop a little intimacy with you just so that, after take-off, when they take over the armrest you share, you'll feel embarrassed enough to let them have it. 'My first time in America,' the albino said. 'I've heard that the police there are completely crazy. They'll throw you in jail just for jaywalking.' 'It'll be fine,' Gershon answered curtly and closed his eyes. He pictured himself entering the office of the Global Toys CEO, giving the silver-haired man standing in front of him a warm, firm handshake and saying,

'You have grandchildren, Mr Lipskar? Let me tell you what they'll be playing this summer.' His left leg kept banging against the side of the plane. He had to remember not to jiggle his legs during the meeting, he told himself, it projects a lack of confidence.

He didn't touch the meal they served on the plane. The albino devoured the chicken and the salad as if they were gourmet food. Gershon glanced at his tray again. It all looked bad. The clingfilm-wrapped chocolate cake reminded him of the dog shit in his wife's dream. But the apple looked relatively OK. He wrapped it in a napkin and put it in his completely empty briefcase. I should have put a few brochures in there, he thought, what if my suitcase doesn't arrive?

We're All Human

It didn't. All the passengers, including the albino, had already gone. The empty luggage carousel revolved for another few minutes, then got tired and stopped. One of the Continental ground staff said that she was very sorry and wrote down his hotel address. 'It's very rare,' she said, 'but mistakes do happen. We're all human, you know.' Maybe. Even though there were moments when Gershon felt he wasn't. For instance, when Eran died in his arms in Laniado Hospital. If Gershon had been human, he probably would have cried or collapsed. People close to him told him that he just hadn't taken it in yet, he needed time; that it wouldn't hit him till he understood it with his heart, not just his brain. But ten years had passed since then and nothing had hit him. In the army, when they wouldn't let him go into officers training, he'd cried like a girl. He remembered how the company's sergeant major had stared at him in helpless shock, but when his best friend died, nothing.

'We will of course compensate you with \$120 against a bill for clothes and personal items,' the woman from Continental said.

'Personal items,' Gershon repeated.

She took the repetition as a question. 'You know, a toothbrush, shaving cream. It's all spelled out on the back of the form.' She pointed to the right place on the page and added, 'I am really and truly sorry.'

A Good One

Standing in the lobby of the Global Toys building was a young man in a cheap suit. A pencil moustache rested not quite naturally above his open mouth, as if his upper lip was embarrassed about something and had decided to wear a toupee. Gershon wanted to ask him where the lift was, but a second later, spotted it himself. He knew that Mr Lipskar would consider him unprofessional because he had no brochures. He should have thought about that in advance and at least packed the presentation in his hand luggage. He probably would have if that annoying dream of his wife's hadn't been bouncing around in the space of his skull while he was packing. 'ID, please,' the Moustache said, and Gershon replied, surprised, 'Excuse me?' 'An ID,' the Moustache repeated, and said to the bald black guy in the grey jacket standing next to him, 'You see the kind of characters we get here?'

Gershon went through his pockets slowly. In Israel he was used to always showing identification, but this was the first time someone outside the country had asked him for anything like that, and somehow, Moustache's tough New York accent made it sound as if, in another second, he'd handcuff him and read him his rights. 'They take their time, don't they?' Moustache said to the black guy in the jacket. 'Why not,' Jacket smiled a soft, yellow smile, 'we're here anyway.' 'What can I tell you, Patrick,' Moustache said, glancing at the passport Gershon handed him, 'your mother didn't name you Patrick for nothing. You're a saint.' He handed the passport back to Gershon and mumbled something. Gershon nodded and started walking towards the lift. 'Hold on,' Moustache said, 'where are you running to? Hey, you, don't you understand English?' 'Actually I do understand English,' Gershon answered impatiently, 'and if you don't mind, I'm in a hurry to get to a meeting.' 'I asked you to open your briefcase, Mr Actually-I-do-understand-English,' Moustache imitated Gershon's Israeli accent, 'Will you do that for me?' And he said to Jacket, who was standing next to him, having the time of his life, trying not to smile, 'I'm telling you, it's a zoo in here.' Gershon thought about the half-eaten apple in his empty briefcase. He tried to imagine the Moustache's smart-arse reaction when he saw it, and Jacket next to him losing the battle to control himself and bursting out laughing. 'Well, open it already,' Moustache continued, 'you know what "open" means, sir?' And quickly spelled the word. 'I know what "open" means,' Gershon replied, clutching the case to his chest with both hands. 'I also know what "closed" means, and "nominal yield" and "oxymoron". I even know the second law of thermodynamics and what Wittgenstein's tractatus is. I know lots of things you'll never know, you arrogant little nothing. And one of those amazing secrets you'll never get to host under the very thin skin of your brain is what I have in my briefcase. Do you even know who I am? Why I came here today? Do you even know anything about existence? The world? Anything beyond the number of the bus that takes you here and home every day, beyond the names of the neighbours in that dark, crappy building you live in?' 'Sir . . .' Jacket tried to stop his flow with pragmatic politeness, but it was too late. 'I look at you,' Gershon went on, 'and in a second I see your whole life story. Everything's written right there, on that receding hairline of yours. Everything. The best day of your life will be when the basketball team you support wins the championship. The worst day will be when your fat wife dies of cancer because your medical insurance doesn't cover the treatment. And everything that comes between those two moments will pass like a weak fart so that at the end of your life, when you try to look back, you won't even be able to remember what it smells like . . .'

Gershon didn't even have time to feel the fist connect with his face. When he came to, he found himself on the lobby's elegant marble floor. What revived him was a series of kicks to the ribs and a deep, pleasant voice echoing in the space of the lobby that reminded him a little of a late-night radio announcer's voice. 'Let it go,' the voice repeated, 'let it go, Jesus, he's not worth it.'

He noticed now that embedded in the floor were small gold stones forming the letter 'G' – the first letter of his first name. He could have put it down to coincidence, but Gershon chose to imagine that the workmen who built this skyscraper knew that he'd come here one day and wanted to make some kind of gesture in his honour so he wouldn't feel so alone and unwanted in this evil city. The kicks didn't stop and they felt so real, just like his wife's dream. Maybe the baby girl her father left in the pram was actually her. Could be. After all, her father was kind of a shit. Maybe that's why the dream was so important to her. And if she'd needed a hug in the dream, he could have hugged her. He could have taken a second's break from his fucking struggle with the traitorous suitcase, which at this very moment was probably sniffing strangers' ankles on a carousel in some tiny airport on the West Coast, held her tightly in his arms and told her, 'I'm here, sweetheart, I may be flying today but I'll be back soon.'

The black guy in the grey jacket helped him up. 'You OK, sir?' he asked and handed him his case and a tissue. 'You're bleeding a little.' He said the words 'a little' in a gentle, muted voice, as if he were trying to shrink it to the size of a drop. Moustache was sitting on a chair near the lift, crying. 'I apologise for him,' Jacket said, 'he's going through a tough time right now.' The word 'tough' he enlarged. Almost shouted. 'Don't apologise,' Moustache said through his tears, 'don't say you're sorry to that bastard.' Jacket began shrugging and sniffling helplessly. 'His mother . . .' he tried to whisper to Gershon. 'Don't tell him,' Moustache

179

wept, 'don't you say a word about my mother, you hear? Or I'll let you have a good one too.'

Rorschach

'Stop—Police,' Gershon went on, 'might be the first board game in history that doesn't impose solutions on the child playing it but stimulates him to find his own solutions. You can think of the game as a sort of path of Rorschach blots that encourage you to use your imagination as you progress towards your goal – to win.' 'A path of Rorschach blots.' Mr Lipskar gave a crooked smile. 'Amazing. I like it, Mr Arazi. But are you sure you're really all right?' 'I'm fine,' Gershon nodded. 'With your permission, could we perform a small simulation of the game now?' 'Simulation,' Mr Lipskar repeated. He was a lot younger than Gershon had imagined, not a trace of grey in his shiny black hair. 'I'm sorry, but I don't think this is the right time for that. Your eye. And your nose. My God, so much blood! Who did this to you?'

What, of this Goldfish, Would You Wish?

Yonatan had a brilliant idea for a documentary. He'd knock on doors. Just him. No camera crew, no nonsense. Just Yonatan, on his own, a small camera in hand, asking, 'If you found a talking goldfish that granted you three wishes, what would you wish for?'

People would give their answers, and Yoni would edit them down and make clips of the more surprising responses. Before every set of answers, you'd see the person standing stock-still in the entrance to his house. Onto this shot he'd super-impose the subject's name, family situation, monthly income, and maybe even the party he'd voted for in the last election. All that, combined with the three wishes, and maybe he'd end up with a poignant piece of social commentary, a testament to the massive rift between our dreams and the often compromised reality in which we live.

It was genius, Yoni was sure. And, if not, at least it was cheap. All he needed was a door to knock on and a heart beating on the other side. With some decent footage, he was sure he'd be able to sell it to Channel 8 or Discovery in a flash, either as a film or as a collection of vignettes, little cinematic corners, each with that singular soul standing in a doorway, followed by three killer wishes, precious, every one.

Even better, maybe he'd sell out, package it with a slogan and flog it to a bank or mobile phone company. Maybe tag it with something like, 'Different dreams, different wishes, one bank.' Or, 'The bank that makes dreams come true.'

No prep, no plotting, natural as can be, Yoni grabbed his camera and went out knocking on doors. In the first neighbourhood he went to, the nice people that took part generally requested the obvious things: health, money, bigger flats, to shave off either a couple of years or a couple of pounds. But there were also powerful moments. One drawn, wizened old lady asked simply for a child. A Holocaust survivor with a number on his arm asked very slowly, in a quiet voice – as if he'd been waiting for Yoni to come, as if it wasn't an exercise at all – he'd been wondering (if this fish didn't mind), would it be possible for all the Nazis left living in the world to be held accountable for their crimes? A cocky, broad-shouldered ladykiller put out his cigarette and, as if the camera wasn't there, wished he were a girl. 'Just for a night,' he added, holding a single finger right up to the lens.

And these were wishes from just one short block in one small, sleepy suburb of Tel Aviv. Yonatan could hardly imagine what people were dreaming of in the development towns and the collectives along the northern border, in the West Bank settlements and Arab villages, the immigrant absorption centres full of broken trailers and tired people left to fry out in the desert sun.

Yonatan knew that if the project was going to have any weight, he'd have to get to everyone, to the unemployed, to the ultra-religious, to the Arabs and Ethiopians and American ex-pats. He began to plan a shooting schedule for the coming days: Yaffo, Dimona, Ashdod, Sderot, Taibe, Talpiot. Maybe Hebron even. If he could sneak past the wall, Hebron would be great. Maybe somewhere in that city some beleaguered Arab man would stand in his doorway and, looking through Yonatan and his camera, looking out into nothingness, just pause for a minute, nod his head and wish for peace – that would be something to see.

Sergei Goralick doesn't much like strangers banging on his door. Especially when those strangers are asking him questions. In Russia, when Sergei was young, it happened a lot. The KGB felt right at home knocking on his door. His father had been a Zionist, which was pretty much an invitation for them to pop over any old time.

When Sergei got to Israel and then moved to Yaffo, his family couldn't get their heads round it. They'd ask him, What are you hoping to find in a place like that? There's no one there but addicts and Arabs and pensioners. But what is most excellent about addicts and Arabs and pensioners is that they don't come round knocking on Sergei's door. That way Sergei can get his sleep, and get up when it's still dark. He can take his little boat out into the sea and fish until he's finished fishing. By himself. In silence. The way it should be. The way it was.

Until one day some kid with a ring in his ear,

looking a little bit homosexual, comes knocking. Hard like that – rapping at his door. Just the way Sergei doesn't like. And he says, this kid, that he has some questions he wants to put on the TV.

Sergei tells the boy, tells him in what he thinks is a straightforward manner, that he doesn't want it. Not interested. Sergei gives the camera a shove, to help make it clear. But the earring boy is stubborn. He says all kinds of things, fast things. And it's hard for Sergei to follow; his Hebrew isn't great.

The boy slows down, tells Sergei he has a strong face, a nice face, and that he simply has to have him for this film. Sergei can also slow down, he can also make it clear. He tells the boy to fuck off. But the boy is slippery and somehow between saying no and pushing the door closed, Sergei finds that the boy is in his house. He's already making his film, running his camera without any permission, and from behind the camera he's still telling Sergei about his face, that it's full of feeling, that it's tender. Suddenly the boy spots Sergei's goldfish flitting around in its big glass jar in his kitchen.

The kid with the earring starts screaming, 'Goldfish, goldfish,' he's so excited. And this, this really pressures Sergei, who tells the boy, it's nothing, just a normal goldfish, stop filming it. Just a goldfish, Sergei tells him, just something he found flapping around in the net, a deep-sea goldfish. But the boy isn't listening. He's still filming and getting closer and saying something about talking and fish and a magic wish.

Sergei doesn't like this, doesn't like that the boy is almost at it, already reaching for the jar. In this instant Sergei understands the boy hasn't come for television, what he's come for, specifically, is to snatch Sergei's fish, to steal it away. Before the mind of Sergei Goralick really understands what it is his body has done, he seems to have taken the pan off the stove and hit the boy on the head. The boy falls. The camera falls with him. The camera breaks open on the floor, along with the boy's skull. There's a lot of blood coming out of the head, and Sergei really doesn't know what to do.

That is, he knows exactly what to do, but it really would complicate things. Because if he takes this kid to the hospital, people are going to ask what happened, and it would take things in a direction Sergei doesn't want to go.

'No reason to take him to the hospital anyway,'

says the goldfish, in Russian. 'That one's already dead.'

'He can't be dead,' Sergei says, with a moan. 'I barely touched him. It's only a pan. Only a little thing.' Sergei holds it up to the fish, taps it against his own skull to prove it. 'It's not even that hard.'

'Maybe not,' says the fish. 'But, apparently, it's harder than that kid's head.'

'He wanted to take you from me,' Sergei says, almost crying.

'Nonsense,' the fish says. 'He was only here to make a little thing for TV.'

'But he said –'

'He said,' says the fish, interrupting, 'exactly what he was doing. But you didn't get it. Honestly, your Hebrew, it's terrible.'

'And yours is better?' Sergei says. 'Yours is so great?'

'Yes. Mine's super-great,' the goldfish says, sounding impatient. 'I'm a magic fish. I'm fluent in everything.' All the while the puddle of blood from the earring boy's head is getting bigger and bigger and Sergei is on his toes, up against the kitchen wall, desperate not to step in it, not to get blood on his feet.

'You do have one wish left,' the fish reminds Sergei. He says it simply like that, as if Sergei doesn't know – as if either of them ever loses count.

'No,' Sergei says. He's shaking his head from side to side. 'I can't,' he says. 'I've been saving it. Saving it for something.'

'For what?' the fish says.

But Sergei won't answer.

That first wish, Sergei used up when they discovered a cancer in his sister. A lung cancer, the kind you don't get better from. The fish undid it in an instant – the words barely out of Sergei's mouth. The second wish Sergei used up five years ago, on Sveta's boy. The kid was still small then, barely three, but the doctors already knew. Something in her son's head wasn't right. He was going to grow big but not in the brain. Three was about as clever as he'd get. Sveta cried to Sergei in bed all night. Sergei walked home along the beach when the sun came up, and he called to the fish, asked the goldfish to fix it as soon as he'd crossed through the door. He never told Sveta. And a few months later she left him for some policeman, a Moroccan with a shiny Honda. In his heart, Sergei kept telling himself it wasn't for Sveta that he'd done it, that he'd wished his wish purely for the boy. In his mind, he was less sure, and all kinds of thoughts about other things he could have done with that wish continued to gnaw at him, driving him half mad. The third wish, Sergei hadn't yet wished for.

'I can restore him,' says the goldfish. 'I can bring him back to life.'

'No one's asking,' Sergei says.

'I can bring him back to the moment before,' the goldfish says. 'To before he knocks on your door. I can put him back to right there. I can do it. All you need to do is ask.'

'To wish my wish,' Sergei says. 'My last.'

The fish swishes his fish tail back and forth in the water, the way he does, Sergei knows, when he's truly excited. The goldfish can already taste freedom. Sergei can see it in him.

After the last wish, Sergei won't have a choice. He'll have to let the goldfish go. His magic goldfish. His friend.

'Fixable,' Sergei says. 'I'll just mop up the blood. A good sponge and it'll be like it never happened.'

That tail just goes back and forth, the fish's head steady.

Sergei takes a deep breath. He steps out into the middle of the kitchen, out into the puddle. 'When I'm fishing, while it's dark and the world's asleep,' he says, half to himself and half to the fish, 'I'll tie the kid to a rock and dump him in the sea. Not a chance, not in a million years, of anyone ever finding him.'

'You killed him, Sergei,' the goldfish says. 'You murdered someone – but you're not a murderer.' The goldfish stops swishing his tail. 'If, on this, you won't waste a wish, then tell me, Sergei, what is it good for?'

It was in Bethlehem, actually, that Yonatan found his Arab, a handsome man who used his first wish to ask for peace. His name was Munir; he was fat with a big white moustache. Really photogenic. It was moving, the way he said it. Perfect, the way in which Munir wished his wish. Yoni just knew even as he was filming that this man would be his promo.

Either him or that Russian. The one with the faded tattoos that Yoni had met in Yaffo. The one that looked straight into the camera and said, if he ever found a talking goldfish he wouldn't ask of it a single thing. He'd just stick it on a shelf in a big glass jar and talk to him all day, it didn't matter about what. Maybe sports, maybe politics, whatever a goldfish was interested in chatting about.

Anything, the Russian said, not to be alone.

Not Completely Alone

Three of the guys she'd been out with tried to commit suicide. She said that sadly but with a little bit of pride too. One of them even succeeded, jumped off the roof of the university humanities building and smashed his insides into thousands of pieces. On the outside he looked whole, even serene. She didn't go to the university that day but friends told her. Sometimes, when she's at home alone, she can actually feel him there in the living room with her, looking at her, and when that happens, it's scary for a minute, but it makes her happy too. Because she knows she's not completely alone. As for me, she really likes me. Likes but isn't attracted. And that makes her sad, as sad as it makes me, maybe even more. Because she'd really like to be attracted to someone like me. Someone intelligent, someone gentle, someone who really loves her. She's been having an affair for a year with an older art dealer. He's married, doesn't plan to leave his wife, it's not even an option. He's someone she's actually attracted to. It's cruel. Cruel for me and cruel for her. Life would be much simpler if she were attracted to me.

She lets me touch her. Sometimes, when her back hurts, she even asks me to. When I massage her muscles she closes her eyes and smiles. 'That feels good,' she says, 'really good.' Once we even had sex. In retrospect, it was a mistake, she says. Some part of her wanted so much for it to work that she ignored her senses. My smell, my body, something between us just didn't click. She's been studying psychology for four years now and she still can't explain it. How her mind wants to so much but her body just won't go along with it. Thinking about that night we went to bed together makes her sad. Lots of things make her sad. She's an only child. She spent a large part of her childhood alone. Her dad got ill, then was dying, then died. There was no brother to understand her, to console her. I'm the closest thing she has to a brother. Me and Kuti, that's the name of the guy who jumped off the roof of humanities. She can sit and talk to me for hours about anything. She can sleep in the same bed with me, see me naked, be naked around me. Nothing between us embarrasses her. Not even when I masturbate next to her. Even though it stains the sheets and makes her sad. Makes her sad that she can't love me, but if it takes the edge off it for me, then she has no problem washing out the stains.

She and her dad were close before he died. She and Kuti were close too, he was in love with her. I'm the only guy close to her who's still alive. In the end, I'll start going out with another girl and she'll remain alone. It's bound to happen, she knows. And when it does, she'll be sad. Sad for herself, but also happy for me, that I found love. After I come, she strokes my face and says that even though it's sad, it's also flattering to her. Flattering that of all the girls in the world, she's the only one I think about when I masturbate. That art dealer she's sleeping with, he's hairy and shorter than me, but my god is he sexy. He served under Netanyahu in the army, and they've been in touch ever since. Real friends. Sometimes, when the art dealer comes to see her, he tells his wife he's going to Bibi's. Once she bumped into him and his wife in the shopping centre. They were standing a few feet away from each other, she gave him a small, secret smile and he ignored her. His eyes were on her but they were completely blank, as if she were nothing. As if she were invisible. And she understood that he couldn't smile back with his wife standing right there, or say anything to her, but even so, there was something very hurtful about it. She stood there by herself next to the payphones and started to cry. That was the same night she slept with me. In retrospect, it was a mistake.

Four of the guys she'd been out with tried to commit suicide. Two even succeeded. And they were the ones she cared about most. They were close to her, very close, like real brothers. Sometimes when she's alone at home she can actually feel us, Kuti and me, in the living room with her, looking at her. And when that happens, it's scary but it makes her happy too. Because she knows she's not completely alone.

One Step Beyond

Killers for hire, they're like wildflowers. They pop up in more species than you can name. I used to know one who called himself Maximillian Sherman, though I'm sure he had other aliases too. Max was one of those top-tier, high-end sorts of killers. Classy. The type that seals a deal maybe once or twice a year. And with the price he got per scalp, he didn't need to sign on for any more.

My man Maximillian had gone vegetarian at the age of fourteen. He told me it was for reasons of conscience. He'd also adopted a kid from Darfur – a boy called Nuri. Max never once met the kid, but he'd write him long letters, and then Nuri would write him back and shove some photos in the envelope for good measure. What I'm trying to say is, Maximillian was a compassionate killer. He wouldn't murder children. Also, he had a problem with old ladies. That kind of high-mindedness cost him a lot of money over the course of his career. A whole lot of money.

So there's Maximillian, and then there's me. And that's what's lovely about this world of ours, that it's such a rich tapestry. I don't sound all polished like Maximillian. And you won't ever catch me with my nose buried in some scientific paper about toxins that can't be traced in the blood. But, in contrast to Mr Sherman, I am willing to butcher up an old lady. I'll kill children by the pound. And I'll do it without stuttering or blinking, and at no extra charge.

My lawyer says that's exactly why they stuck me with the death penalty. Today, he says, it's not like it used to be. In the old days folks preferred a public hanging over a good meal. These days people have lost their taste for killing murderers. It makes them sick to their stomachs, makes them feel bad about themselves. But child killers? Those they still go after with gusto. Maybe you can make sense of it. As far as I can tell, a life is a life. And Maximillian Sherman and my righteous jurors can screw up their faces until the cows come home, but taking the life of a bulimic twenty-six-year-old student majoring in gender studies, or a sixty-eight-year-old limousine driver who fancies a bit of poetry on the side, that's no more or less all right than snuffing out the life of a runny-nosed three-year-old. Prosecutors love to split hairs over this. They love to mess with your head talking about purity and helplessness. But a life is a life. And as a guy who's stood over plenty of corrupt lawyers and dirty politicians in his day, I've got to stress that at the appointed moment, the instant that the body gives a flutter and the eyes flip in their holes – right then, everyone is innocent and everyone helpless, not a lick of difference. But go and explain that to some half-deaf retired jurist from Miami whose experience of loss – apart from a husband she couldn't much stand – was nursing a pet hamster named Charlie as he succumbed to a case of cancer in his teeny-tiny colon.

In court they alleged that I am a hater of children. Maybe there's something to that. They dug up an old incident wherein I murdered a set of twins that weren't in the contract. It wasn't pro bono or anything, they just got caught up in the mix. And it's not that I've got any problem with kids when it comes to, say, their outward appearance. Because kids – in appearance – are actually pretty sweet. Like people, but small. They remind me of those mini cans of soda and eensy-weensy boxes of cereal that they used to hand out on planes. But behaviour-wise? I'm sorry. I'm not exactly a fan of their little tantrums and break-downs, the hysterics on the floor in the middle of the shopping mall. All that screeching, with the Daddy-go-away's and I-don't-love-Mummy's – and all because of some shitty two-dollar toy that, even if you buy it for them, won't get played with for more than a minute. I even hate the whole bedtime-story bit. It's not just the awkward situa-tion where you're forced to lie next to them in their little uncomfortable beds, or that emotional blackmail of theirs. And, trust me, they don't hold back, they'll roll you over a barrel to get another story out of you, but, for me, the worst part is the stories themselves. Always precious, with sweet woodsy creatures stripped of their fangs and claws; illustrated lies about worlds without evil, places more boring than death. And if we're back on the subject of death: my lawyer thinks we can appeal the sentence. Not that it'll help. But making sure this whole performance reaches a higher court would buy us some time. I told him I'm not interested. Between you and me, what would I get from that little slice of living? More push-ups in a six-by-nine cell? More college basketball and crappy reality TV? If the only thing I've got coming down the pipeline is a needle full of poison, let them stick me now and move on. Let's not drag our feet.

When I was a kid, my father was always yammering on about Heaven. He talked about it so much that he completely lost sight of who, in this world, my mother was fucking behind his back. If my father's take on the world to come is right, then it'll be anything but boring to be there. He was Jewish, my father. But in prison, when they ask me, I request myself a priest. Somehow, those Christians just seem a little less abstract to me. And in my situation, the philosophical angle isn't exactly relevant. What's important right now is the practical. That I'll end up in Hell is a given, and the more information I manage to draw out of the priest, the better prepared I'll be when I get there. I'm speaking from experience when I tell you, there's no place where crushing a kneecap or a caving in a skull won't increase your social standing. It doesn't matter if it's a reform school in Georgia, basic training in the Marines, or a closed prison wing in Bangkok. The wisdom is in being able to identify on who, exactly, to crush what. And this is precisely where the priest was supposed to help. In retrospect, I see I could've requested a rabbi or a cadi or even a mute Hindu baba, because that chatterbox priest hasn't helped at all. He looks exactly like a Japanese tourist and must know it, because the first thing he rushes to tell me is that he's already a fourth-generation American, which is more than you can say for me. The priest says that Hell is completely personal. Exactly like Heaven. And in the end, everyone gets the Hell or the Heaven he deserves. Still, I won't give up. Who's in charge there? I ask him. How does it work? Is there any history of people that manage to escape? But he won't answer, just nods his head up and down like those dogs you stick on the dashboard. By the third time he asks me to give confession, I can't take it any more and I pop him real good. My hands and my legs are restrained when I do it, so I've got to use my head. The nut is more than enough. I don't know what materials they use to build

Japanese priests nowadays, but mine came apart in an instant.

The guards that separate us beat me something serious: kicking, and clubbing, landing punches to the head. They act as if they're trying to subdue me, but they're just beating me silly for the hell of it. I understand them. It's fun to hit. The truth? I enjoyed that headbutt to the priest more than the steak and fries they gave me for my last meal, and that prison steak wasn't half bad. It's great fun to hit – and I can only imagine what violence awaits me on the far side of my shot of poison. I promise you that as much as it will be unpleasant for me in Hell, it'll be worse for the son of a bitch standing within reach. And it won't matter to me if the guy's a run-of-the-mill sinner, or a demon, or Satan himself. That bleeding Japanese priest got my appetite going.

The needle hurts. They definitely could've found one that didn't, those self-righteous puritans, but they chose one with sting. They do it to punish.

While I'm dying, I remember everyone I killed. I see the expressions that spread over their faces right before their souls escaped through their ears. It's possible that they'll all be waiting there, seething, on the other side. Right then I feel one final, massive spasm take over my body, like someone's just closed a fist tight around my heart. My victims? Let them wait for me. I hope they're there! It'll be a pleasure to kill them all again.

I open my eyes. There's high green grass around me, like in the jungle. Somehow I imagined a Hell more basement-like, all dark and dungeony. But here everything's green and the sun is high in the sky and dazzling. I forge a path forward, searching the ground for something I can use as a weapon: a stick, a stone, a sharpened branch. There's nothing. Nothing around me but tall grass and damp ground. That's when I notice a pair of giant human legs nearby. Whoever he is, he's eight times my size – and like me completely unarmed. I'll need to find his weak spots: knee, balls, windpipe. I'll need to hit hard and hit fast and pray that it works. That's when the giant bends down. He's more agile than I expected. He plucks me into the air with force, and his mouth opens. Here you are, he says, and he holds me against his chest. Here you are, my sweet little bear. You know I love you more than anything in the world! I try to take advantage of our proximity, try to bite him on the neck, to shove a finger in his eye. I want to, but my body doesn't listen. It moves against my wishes, and there I am hugging him back. Then it's the lips moving, beyond my control. They part and they whisper, I love you too, Christopher Robin. I love you more than anyone in the world.

Big Blue Bus

Some children throw themselves on the floor and have a tantrum. They cry and flail their arms and squirm till their faces turn red and sweaty and the saliva and mucus that drip out of their mouths and their noses start to stain the grey stone of the pavement. Be grateful he's not one of those.

Gilad clung to that thought in an attempt to calm himself. That thought and slow breathing. And it helped. On the pavement beside him was little Hillel, his fists clenched, his forehead wrinkled, his eyes shut tight and his mouth whispering over and over again the same words, like a mantra: 'I want to I want to I want to.'

Gilad decides to smile before he starts talking. He knows Hillel can't actually see the smile, but hopes that somehow, something of the smile will carry over in his voice. 'Hillel, my sweet,' he says through the smile, 'Hillel, my precious, let's start walking before it's too late. They're having pancakes for breakfast at nursery today and unless we get there on time the other children will finish everything and won't leave you any.'

I want to I want to I want to I want to I want to
I want to I want to I want to I want to I want to

Before he and Naama split up they had a rule about Hillel not watching television. Naama was the one who started it. She'd read something in *Haaretz*, and Gilad followed through with it. It seemed to make sense. But after they split up they weren't there any more to monitor each other. All in all, when you're on your own, it's harder to be consistent. Every time you give in you feel like the other parent is the one who's going to have to pay for it later on, or at least to split the bill with you, and suddenly the cost seems more tolerable. A bit like throwing a cigarette butt on the stairway v. throwing it inside your own home. And now that they don't have a home any more, meaning that they don't have the same one, they're chucking them all over the place.

I want to I want to I want to I want to I want to
I want to I want to I want to I want to I want to
One of the programmes Hillel loves watching
when he's with Gilad is a Japanese cartoon series
about a little boy with magic powers, whose
name is Tony. This boy's mother, who is a fairy,
taught him once that if he just closed his eyes
and kept saying 'I want to', all his wishes would
come true. Sometimes it takes less than a second
for Tony's dream to come true, and if that
doesn't happen, his mother the fairy explains
that it isn't because he's failed but simply because
he stopped saying 'I want to' too soon. Tony
could go through almost a whole episode with
his eyes closed and 'I want to I want to I want
to' without giving up, until the magic worked.
As far as the production costs were concerned,
the idea was very economical, because in every
show you could recycle the shot with Tony, the
bead of sweat gleaming on his forehead,
mumbling over and over again 'I want to I want
to I want to'. The same shot, over and over, in
every episode. You could go mad just sitting
there and watching it, but Hillel can't take his
eyes off the screen.

I want to I want to I want to I want to I want to
I want to I want to I want to I want to I want to
Gilad is smiling again. 'It won't do any good, Hilleli,' he says. 'Even if you say it a million times, it won't do any good. We can't take the bus to nursery because it's just too close. It's just here, at the end of the road. And there's no bus that goes there.'

'It will too,' Hillel says and even though he's stopped droning, his eyes stay shut, and his forehead stays wrinkled. 'Really, Daddy. It will. I just stopped too soon.' Gilad was about to take advantage of the window of opportunity in the droning to sneak in a tempting proposition. A bribe. A Snickers bar maybe. There's a shop right next to the nursery. Naama doesn't allow chocolate bars in the morning, but he doesn't care now. Naama won't allow it, and Gilad will. There are extenuating circumstances. The thoughts rush through his mind, but before Gilad has a chance to offer the Snickers bar, Hillel is at it again.

I want to I want to I want to I want to I want to
I want to I want to I want to I want to I want to
Gilad announces the Snickers. He repeats this

several times. Snickers. Snickers. Snick-ers. At the top of his voice. Close to Hillel's ear. If Naama were there, she'd tell Gilad to stop shouting at him and she'd look horrified. That's something she's good at – looking horrified. Making him feel at any given moment that he's an abusive father or a terrible husband or just a crap human being. And that's a kind of talent too. A magical power. Weak magic, true, weak and nerve-wracking, but still it's magic. And what magic powers can Gilad display? None. One magican mother, one magician child, one father with no powers at all. A Japanese series. It can go on like this forever.

I want to I want to I want to I want to I want to
I want to I want to I want to I want to I want to

Gilad holds Hillel tight in both arms, hoists him in the air and starts running. Hillel is warm, the way he always is. Even now, he keeps muttering, but as soon as Gilad starts holding him close the muttering turns calmer and the furrows in his forehead disappear. Gilad feels he ought to be muttering something too, together with Hillel. He starts with 'We're going to nursery we're going to nursery', and halfway there he shifts to 'We'll be there soon we'll be there soon we'll be there soon', and when they're really close to the playground and to the locked electric gate it suddenly turns into 'Daddy loves Daddy loves Daddy loves'. It has nothing to do with anything, and the sentence doesn't have an object even though it's obvious, to Gilad at least, that he means he loves Hillel.

As they enter the nursery, he stops muttering and puts Hillel down on the ground. Hillel continues, his eyes shut: 'I want to I want to I want to.' Gilad smiles at one of the teaching assistants, a chubby lady he happens to like, and hangs Hillel's embroidered bag, with the extra set of clothes and the plastic bottle, on the hook where it says HILLEL in bold print. He begins making his way out when the teacher stops him.

I want to I want to I want to I want to I want to
I want to I want to I want to I want to I want to

Gilad smiles at her. He's perspiring after the run and panting a bit too, but his smile says everything is fine. 'It's something Hillel saw on television last night,' he explains. 'This series —

Tony and the magic butterflies. Something Japanese. Children love it . . .' The teacher shushes him the way he's seen her do with misbehaving children. It's insulting, but he prefers not to react. All he wants is to get out of there. And the calmer and nicer he is – he thinks – the sooner he'll be able to leave. And he can always tell the teacher about some meeting at the office or something. After all, she knows he's a lawyer.

I want to I want to I want to I want to I want to
I want to I want to I want to I want to I want to

The teacher tries to talk to Hillel. She even touches him on the face gently, but Hillel doesn't stop muttering and doesn't open his eyes. Gilad's instinct is to tell her it won't do any good, but he's not sure this is going to work in his favour. Maybe now, he thinks to himself, maybe now is the right moment to mention the meeting at the office and to simply leave.

I want to I want to I want to I want to I want to
I want to I want to I want to I want to I want to

'I'm sorry,' the teacher says, 'you can't leave him here in this state.' Gilad tries to explain it's not a state. It's just some rubbish they show on television, it's like a game. It isn't like the child is suffering or anything. He's just obsessed with this nonsense. But the teacher won't listen and Gilad has no choice other than to pick Hillel up again. The teacher walks them out, and as she opens the gate for them she says in an empathic tone that it might be a good idea to phone Naama because this isn't something they can ignore, and Gilad agrees with her at once and says he'll take care of it, mainly because he's afraid she'll call Naama herself.

I want to I want to I want to I want to I want to
I want to I want to I want to I want to I want to

Once they're outside, Gilad puts Hillel down on the pavement and says in a fairly quiet tone: 'Which bus?' And as Hillel goes right on muttering, he repeats his question louder: 'Which bus?' Hillel stops, opens his eyes, gives Gilad a penetrating look and says: 'A big blue bus.' Gilad nods and trying to sound completely normal, completely without tears, he asks whether it matters which number the bus has. And Hillel smiles and shakes his head.

They walk towards Dizengoff Street and wait at the bus stop. The first one that arrives is red. They don't get on. But right after that another one pulls up. It's big and blue. Bus number 1 to Abu Kabir. While Gilad buys the ticket, Hillel waits patiently, the way he promised he would, and then makes his way carefully down the aisle holding onto the poles. They sit down at the back, next to each other. The bus is completely empty. Gilad tries to remember the last time he was in Abu Kabir. It was when he was still doing his internship and someone in the office sent him to the Forensic Institute there to photocopy an autopsy report. That was before he realised that criminal law was not for him. Hillel wants to know if this bus goes to the nursery and Gilad says more or less, or that metaphorically speaking it does, eventually. If Hillel asks what metaphorically means, the way he sometimes does when he comes across words like that, he'll have a problem. But Hillel doesn't ask. He just puts his little hand on Gilad's thigh and looks out the window. Gilad leans back, shuts his eyes and tries not to think about anything. The wind through the open window is strong, but not too strong. His body is breathing slowly and his lips aren't moving at all, but in his heart he keeps saying: 'I want to I want to I want to I want to I want to I want to.'

Haemorrhoid

This is the story of a man who suffered from a haemorrhoid. Not a lot of haemorrhoids. A single, solitary one. This haemorrhoid started out small and annoying, but very soon it became medium-sized and irritating, and in less than two months it grew to be big and really painful. The man continued to live his life as usual: he worked long hours every day, took time off on weekends and got laid whenever he had the chance. But this haemorrhoid, which was clinging to a vein, kept reminding him at every long meeting or through every painful bowel movement that to live is to suffer, to live is to sweat, to live is an ache you can't fucking forget. And so, before every important decision the man would listen to his haemorrhoid the way others listen to their conscience. And the haemorrhoid, like any haemorrhoid, would give the man some arsehole advice. Advice on whom to fire, advice on aiming higher, advice on whether to pick a fight and with whom he should conspire. And it worked. With every passing day, the man became more and more successful. The earnings of the company he ran kept growing, and so did the haemorrhoid. It reached a point where the haemorrhoid outgrew the man. And even then, it didn't stop. Until eventually it was the haemorrhoid that was Chairman of the Board. And sometimes, when the haemorrhoid took its seat on the chair in the boardroom, it found the man underneath a little irritating.

This is the story of a haemorrhoid that suffered from a man. The haemorrhoid continued to live its life as usual: it worked long hours every day, took time off on weekends and get laid whenever it had the chance. But this man, who was clinging to a vein, kept reminding him at every long meeting or painful bowel movement that to live is to yearn, to live is to burn, to live is to fucking screw up and wait for fate to turn. And the haemorrhoid would listen to the man the way people listen to their stomach when it rumbles and asks for food – passively but acceptingly. And thanks to this man, the haemorrhoid tried to believe it could live and let live, it could learn to forgive. It could conquer its urge to look down on others. And even when it swore, it didn't mention people's mothers. And so, thanks to the irritating little man under him, everyone came to value the haemorrhoid: haemorrhoids, people and, of course, the company's satisfied shareholders all around the world.

September All Year Long

When the great depression began, NW was hardest hit. Their merchandise was meant for the affluent class, but after the Chicago riots, even the wealthy stopped ordering, some of them because of the unstable economic situation, but most of them because they just couldn't face their neighbours. The shares lay on the stock market floors of the world and bled out, percentage after percentage. And NW turned into a symbol of the depression. The headline of the *Wall Street Journal*'s story about them was 'HAIL STORMS IN SEPTEMBER', a rip-off of their ad, 'September All Year Long', which showed a family clad only in bathing suits on a sunny autumn day decorating a Christmas tree. The advert caught on like wildfire. A week after it was broadcast for the first time, they were already selling three thousand units a day. Wealthy

Americans bought, and so did the less wealthy who were faking it. The NW weather control systems became a status symbol. The official stamp of a millionaire. They now signified what private jets used to signify in the nineties and into 2000. Nice Weather, weather for the wealthy. If you live in arctic Greenland, and the snow and greyness are driving you crazy, all you have to do is swipe your credit card and, with a satellite or two, they'll set you up with a perfect autumn day in Cannes on your balcony every day of the year.

Yakov (Yaki) Brayk was one of the first to buy the system from them. He truly loved his money and found parting with it hard, but even more than he loved the millions he earned from selling weapons and drugs to Zimbabwe, he hated those humid New York summers and that icky feeling when your sweaty undershirt sticks to your back. He bought a system not only for himself, but for the whole block. Some people mistakenly saw that as generosity, but the truth is, he did it just to keep the great weather with him all the way to the corner shop. That shop wasn't only the place to buy unfiltered Noblesse cigarettes they imported from Israel for him; more than anything, it marked for Yaki the boundary of his living space. And from the minute Yaki signed the cheque, the block turned into a weather paradise. No dismal rain or sweltering heat. Just September all year long. And not, God forbid, that annoying New York September, but the kind he grew up with in Haifa. And then suddenly, out of the blue, there were the riots in Chicago and the neighbours demanded that he turn off his perfect autumn weather. At first, he ignored them, but then those lawyers' letters turned up in his postbox and someone left a slaughtered peacock on his windshield. That's when his wife asked him to turn it off. It was January. Yaki turned off the autumn and the day instantly became shorter and sadder. All because of one slaughtered peacock and an anxiety-ridden, anorexic wife who, as always, was able to control him through her weakness.

The recession just got worse. On Wall Street, NW stocks hit rock bottom, and so did shares in Yaki's company. And after they hit rock bottom, they drilled a hole through the rocks and fell even lower. It's funny, you'd think that weapons and drugs would be recession-proof, but actually the opposite turned out to be true. People had no money to buy medicine and they rediscovered what they'd long forgotten: that live weapons are a luxury, just like electric car windows, and that sometimes it only takes a stone you found in the yard to smash somebody's skull in. They quickly learned to manage without Yaki's rifles, much more quickly than Yaki could get used to the gloomy weather of mid-March. And Yaki Brayk, or Lucky Brayk, as the financial columnists liked to call him, went bankrupt.

He kept the apartment (the company's accountant managed to retroactively put it in the anorexic's wife's name), but all the rest was gone. They even took the furniture. Four days later, a NW technician came to disconnect the system. When Yaki opened the door for him, he was standing there completely rain-soaked. Yaki made him hot coffee and they talked for a while. Yaki told him that not long after the Chicago riots, he'd stopped using the system. The technician said that a lot of customers had stopped. They talked about the riots, when furious mobs from the slums stormed the summery homes of the wealthy residents of the city. 'All that sun they had drove us crazy,' one of the rioters said on a news commentary show a few days later. 'Let's see you freezing your butt off with no money for heat and those bastards, those bastards . . .' At that point, he burst into tears. The camera blurred his face to hide his identity, so you couldn't actually see the tears, but you could hear him wailing like a wounded animal. The technician, who was black, said he was born in that neighbourhood in Chicago, but today he was ashamed to admit it. 'That money,' he said, 'all that fucking money just fucked up the world.'

After coffee, when the technician was ready to disconnect the system, Yaki asked if he could turn it on just one last time. The technician shrugged and Yaki took that as a yes. He pressed a few buttons on the remote and the sun suddenly came out from behind a cloud. 'That's not the real sun, you know,' the technician said proudly. 'What they do is image it, with lasers.' Yaki winked and said, 'Don't spoil it. For me, it's the sun.' The technician nodded and said, 'A great sun. Too bad you can't keep it out till I get back to the car. I'm sick of this rain.' Yaki didn't answer. He just closed his eyes and let the sun wash over his face.

Joseph

There are conversations that can change a person's life. I'm sure of it. I mean, I'd like to believe it. I'm sitting in a cafe with a producer. He's not exactly a producer, he's never produced anything, but he wants to. He has an idea for a film and he wants me to write the screenplay. I explain that I don't write for films and he accepts that and calls the waitress over. I'm sure he wants to ask for the bill, but he orders himself another espresso instead. The waitress asks me if I want something else and I ask for a glass of water. The wannabe producer's name is Yossef, but he introduces himself as Joseph. 'No one,' he says, 'is really called Yossef. It's always Sefi or Yossi or Yoss, so I went for Joseph.' He's sharp, that Joseph. Reads me like a book. 'You're busy, aren't you?' he says when he sees me glance at my watch, and immediately adds, 'Very busy. Travelling, working, writing emails.' There's nothing malicious or sarcastic in the way he says it. It's a statement of fact or, at the most, an expression of sympathy. I nod. 'Not being busy scares you?' he asks. I nod again. 'Me too,' he says and gives me a yellow-toothed smile. 'There must be something down there. Something frightening. If not, we wouldn't be grinding our time so thin on all kinds of projects. And you know what scares me most?' he asks. I hesitate for a second, thinking about what to answer, but Joseph doesn't wait. 'Myself,' he continues, 'what I am. You know that nothingness that fills you up a second after you come? Not with someone you love, just with some girl, or when you have a wank. You know? That's what scares me, looking into myself and finding nothing there. Not your average nothingness, but the kind that totally does your head in, I don't know exactly what to call it . . .'

Now he's quiet. I feel uncomfortable with his silence. If we were closer, maybe I could be silent with him. But not at our first meeting. Not after a comment like that. 'Sometimes,' I try to return his frankness, 'life seems like a trap to me.

Something you walk into unsuspectingly and then it snaps closed around you. And when you're inside, inside life I mean, there's no escape, except maybe suicide, which isn't really an escape, it's more like surrender. You know what I mean?'

'It's fuck all,' Joseph says. 'It's just fuck all that you won't write the screenplay.' There's something very weird about the way he talks. He doesn't even swear like other people. I don't know what to say after that, so I keep quiet. 'Never mind,' he says after a minute. 'Your saying no just gives me the chance to meet other people, drink more coffee. And that's the best part of this business. I don't think the actual producing is for me.' I must have nodded because he reacts to it. 'You think I don't have it, do you? You think that I'm not really a producer, that I'm just some guy with a bit of money from his parents who talks a lot.' I must still be nodding, unintentionally, from the pressure, because now he's laughing. 'You're right,' he says, 'or maybe not, maybe I'll surprise you yet. And myself.'

Joseph asks for the bill and insists on paying. 'What about our waitress?' he asks while we wait for his credit card to be swiped, 'You think she's trying to escape too? From herself, I mean?' I shrug. 'And that guy who just walked in, with the coat? Look how he's sweating. He's definitely running away from something. Maybe we'll form a start-up. Instead of the film – a programme that finds people who are trying to run away from themselves, who are afraid of what they might find out. It could be a hit.' I look at the sweaty guy in the coat. It's the first time in my life I see a suicide bomber. Afterwards, in the hospital, foreign journalists will ask me to describe him and I'll say I don't remember. Because I'll think it's something kind of personal, something I should keep between me and him. Joseph will survive the blast too. But not so the waitress. Not that there's any culpability on her part. In terrorist attacks, character is not a factor. In the end, it's all a matter of angle and distance. 'That guy who just came in is definitely running away from something,' Joseph says and laughs, rummaging around in his pockets for some change for the tip. 'Maybe he'll agree to write the screenplay for me or at least meet for coffee.' Our waitress, laminated menu in hand, dances her way over to the sweaty guy in the coat.

Mourners' Meal

She decided to open the restaurant straightaway, the morning after the funeral. When Itamar heard about it, she thought he'd explode. 'Just one hour ago you buried your husband, and already you're in a hurry to sell çorba?!' 'We don't do çorba, Itamar,' Halina said in her most reassuring voice, 'and it's not about money at all. It's about people. I do better being with customers at the restaurant than sitting at home on my own.' 'But you're the one who insisted we shouldn't sit shiva,' Itamar said. 'You said you didn't want all the hassle.' 'It wasn't because of the hassle,' Halina protested. 'When people leave their body to science, you don't sit shiva. That's just how it is. When Horshovsky's father died, nobody –' 'Give me a break, Mother,' Itamar snapped. 'Leave Horshovsky out of this, and the Shiffermans and

Mrs Pinchevsky from 21 Bialik Street. Just us, OK? Does it seem reasonable to you that the day after Dad dies you go and open the restaurant as if it were business as usual?' 'Yes,' Halina insisted. 'In my heart, it won't be as usual, but for everyone who comes into the restaurant it will be. Your father may be dead, but the business is alive.' 'The business is dead too,' Itamar said, gritting his teeth. 'It's been dead for years now. We haven't had so much as a dog in here.'

At the hospital, when they told her Gideon had died, she didn't cry. But after what Itamar said, she did. Not in front of him, of course; as long as he was around, she kept a stiff upper lip. But as soon as he left, she cried like a baby. 'It doesn't mean I'm not a good wife,' she assured herself between sobs. 'I'm a lot more upset that Gideon is dead than that Itamar said those things, but insults are much easier to cry over.' It was true. Ever since they'd moved to the arcade the book-ings had dwindled. She'd been against the move from the word go, but Gideon said it was their big chance, 'the chance of a lifetime'. Ever since then, every time they argued, she'd remind him of that 'chance of a lifetime', and now that he was dead, there was nobody for her to remind. She and the Chinaman had been sitting in the empty restaurant for three hours in complete silence. The Chinaman had been very fond of Gideon, who was very patient with him. Gideon used to spend hours teaching the Chinaman how to make cholent and gefilte fish, and whenever he ruined anything, and Halina would blurt out a swear word, Gideon would intervene: 'Never mind, never mind.' If nobody turns up by three, I'll close, she thought. Not just for today. For good. Two people running a business is different. When there's a crowd there's someone to help out, and when there isn't, at least you have someone to talk to. 'You OK?' the Chinaman asked, and Halina nodded and tried to smile. Maybe even before three. She'll just lock up and leave.

There were almost twenty of them, and as soon as they stood by the door looking at the menu outside she knew there'd be a racket. The one who came in first was gigantic, a head taller than she was, with salt-and-pepper hair and eyebrows like a carpet. 'You open?' he asked, and for a second she debated, but by the time she'd opened her mouth to answer, the restaurant was packed – with gold-and-purple nail varnish, and the sharp smell of vodka, and shrieking children. She and the Chinaman lined up a few tables, and when she brought them the menus the tall guy said: 'We don't need menus now, lady. Just bring everyone plate and knife-and-fork.' And while she and the Chinaman were setting out the plates she spotted the picnic boxes. They started pulling out food and bottles of drink and filling plates, looking not in the least embarrassed. If Gideon were alive, he'd have kicked them out, but she didn't even have it in her to say anything. 'Now you come here with us,' the tall man said. She signalled the Chinaman to sit down at the table with them, and sat down herself, though she wasn't really in the mood. 'Drink up, lady,' he commanded. 'Drink up.' He filled her glass with vodka. 'Today is special day.' And as she stared at him, puzzled, he added with a wink: 'Today is day we find this restaurant you manage with Japanese guy. Why you not eating?'

Their food was tasty. And after downing a glass or two, Halina didn't mind their coarseness any more. Even if they weren't ordering anything and even if they were using up all the dishes, she was glad they had come, filling the whole place with their shrieking and their laughter. That way at least she didn't have to stay there on her own. They drank l'chaim – to life. To her life, and to the life of the business, and even to the life of Gideon. For some reason that she couldn't quite work out, she told them he was abroad on business. Then they drank to the life of Gideon's business abroad and to Joseph, which was what they called the Chinaman. And to the life of Joseph's family and then to the life of the State. And Halina, who was a bit drunk by then, tried to remember how many years it had been since she'd last toasted the State. When they finished everything in their picnic boxes, the tall guy asked her what she thought of their food, and Halina said it was excellent. 'Very good,' the tall guy smiled. 'I'm happy. And now, we have your menu.' At first, Halina didn't understand what he meant. Maybe because of the vodka. But the tall guy explained right away: 'You sat with us and you ate our food. Now it is time for us to sit with you and eat your food.'

They ordered from the menu as if they hadn't eaten a thing, and ate voraciously. Salads, soups, pot roasts and, afterwards, even dessert. 'Your food is good, lady,' the tall guy said, taking out his wallet to pay. 'Very good. Even better than what we bring.' And when he'd finished counting the notes and putting them on the table, he added: 'Your husband, when he is coming back?' Halina hesitated before answering, and then said it wasn't clear yet and that it all depended on his business over there. 'He left wife behind, alone?' the tall guy said disapprovingly, his voice kind of sad. 'That is not right.' And Halina, who wanted to say everything was fine and that she was managing, really, found herself nodding, and smiling, as if her eyes weren't glistening with tears.

More Life

This is one story you've got to hear! Two identical twin brothers from Jacksonville, Florida, met two identical twin sisters from Daytona Beach. They met through the Internet. Or, to be exact, it started with just one couple, Nicky and Todd, and when Todd brought Nicky home for dinner at his parents' place, his twin brother Adam got really excited. That's when Todd told him she had a sister. Not just a sister, an identical twin. Todd and Nicky set up this blind date. Of course it couldn't exactly be called a blind date, considering that Adam and Michelle both knew what the other person would look like. To make things less awkward, they turned it into a double date and the four of them went to see a movie at the drive-in. And what movie did they go see? No, not *Twins* with Schwarzenegger and DeVito. They went to see *Dangerous Liaisons*. Can you imagine? There couldn't be a worse movie for a blind date, it's all intrigues and cheating and lies, and yet it went well. After the movie they went to a diner. The girls made a point of dressing in different colours so it would be easier to tell them apart. The guys came in jeans and white T-shirts, looking exactly the same. And at one embarrassing point, that she'd still remember years later, Nicky made the mistake of kissing Adam, because she thought he was Todd.

When you meet someone and fall in love, what's the strongest emotion you have? I don't know about you, but what I always feel when that happens is that I'm with someone who's completely unlike anyone else in the world. But when Michelle and Adam were sitting across from each other in the diner, what did they think to themselves? That there was no other man in the world like Adam? That there was nobody else at the table like Michelle? Whatever they may have thought at that moment, in the end it led to marriage. Well, maybe that's wrong, in the end it led to death. But at some stage in between, it led to marriage.

When Michelle and Adam got married, it was

a year after Todd had put a ring on Nicky's finger. Identical twin sisters married to identical twin brothers. I don't know if there's ever been anything like it in all of history. Forget the history of Florida, the history of the world. It was so uncanny, they were even approached by a talk show, and I don't mean some local channel. Someone from NBC. But Michelle said no, because she claimed that if she went on the show she'd feel like a bearded lady. 'I mean, it's not like they're asking us because of anything we did. The only reason they want us on the show is because they think it's weird. I bet they'll tell us to dress the same and they'll start asking Nicky and me why we've got the same haircut, and even if we try to explain it's because that's the haircut that looks best on us, it'll still come out perverted,' she told Adam with great conviction. 'They want us there like some freak show. And I bet the host will make fun of us and tell lots of little jokes and make us look bad. And the audience at home will laugh, and you and Todd will laugh, because you and Todd laugh at everything, and I'll be the only who's dying of embarrassment.' The truth was, Adam would have loved to be on the show. He'd never been on TV, and he knew how impressed the guys at work would be if they saw him on a chat show, and so would the customers. For him, it could have been a laugh, but he didn't even try to reason with her. Because once Michelle had made up her mind, there was no point, she'd never listen to a word that anybody said. In the end, Adam was on TV, and prime time no less, coast to coast. It wasn't exactly in the studio, but they showed him for almost one whole minute in a home video his dad had made years earlier, playing basketball with Todd. It was a scene where he was waving at the camera, and Todd took advantage of it to grab the ball away from him and shoot a basket. 'Even back then,' the announcer in the studio noted, 'you could sense the rivalry between them.' And it wasn't that there had ever been any rivalry, but that's how it is on TV. They love to blow things out of proportion, for dramatic effect. And if they can't find anything to blow out of proportion, they make it up.

In real life, Adam and Todd had actually been on very good terms. Altogether the two couples got along very well. They lived near each other, and spent their weekends with one another. And when they started talking about having families, they even decided to have children at more or less the same time, so they'd grow up together. And those plans would probably have worked out, if it wasn't for what happened. And it's not that anyone suspected anything. Even looking back, it was hard to foresee such a thing. And even if one of the neighbours had happened to see Adam and Nicky kissing on the street or on the porch, they probably took Adam for Todd, or figured that she must be Michelle.

And their affair went on that way for more than a year. At one point, they even thought of coming out with it, telling the whole world, getting divorced and marrying each other. But Nicky knew it would destroy Michelle, and Adam felt sorry for her too, and also for Todd, because even if Todd had hurt him once in the past, maybe more than once, he'd always loved Adam and only wanted what was best for him. Then there was a point when Nicky suggested that they stop. That was when she'd begun to think that Todd might be catching on. Nothing definite, she just had a feeling, and they really did stop seeing each other for a few weeks, but then they got back together, because the separation turned out to be more than either of them could bear.

I only met Nicky a few years after the whole business ended badly. Adam was dead by then, and Todd had already done a lot of time for it. Michelle hadn't spoken a word to Nicky since the whole thing came out, which in her case was on the day Todd put three bullets in Adam's head at point-blank range. Michelle had never exactly been the forgiving type. I had arrived as a guest lecturer at the university and Nicky was the department secretary. I first heard her story from another teacher in the faculty, a guest too, from Turkey, and then from her. She and I ended up getting pretty close that year, and at some stage she told me about it. Even before we slept together.

She said she'd left Florida to get away from it all, but that it hadn't really made a difference because everyone here knew about it too, and they all talked about it behind her back. She said that in some strange way, 'perverse' is what her sister Michelle would probably have called it, she really missed the whole twinhood thing, the way people they'd meet would confuse her with Michelle. 'Somehow,' I remember her telling me, just before we kissed for the first time, 'when you've got an identical twin sister in the same neighbourhood, you feel more. As if you're more than one person and you've got more than one life to live. The very fact that someone tells you "I saw you an hour ago eating vanilla ice cream" or "I saw you at the bus stop in a pink dress" – you can explain it was your sister if you want, but somehow you feel like it really was you having that ice cream or wearing that pink dress. It's a strange feeling, like you're living another life and using your expanded life to do all these mysterious things you'll never really know.' That's not all she missed, she missed her husband too, and above all she missed Adam, a man who was the spitting image – but the absolute spitting image – of her jailed husband, and someone she loved a lot more, even if she couldn't say why.

That night I told her about my own life too, and about my affair. Not with my wife's sister. Just a girl at work who didn't look anything like my wife. She was younger than my wife and much less attractive, but I felt then just like Nicky did, like I was getting myself more life. Not necessarily a better life, not a life more promising than the one I already had. But because I thought this life was in addition and not instead, I devoured it without a second's hesitation. In my case, nobody shot anybody, and even though my wife suspected something, I never got caught. She and I stayed together. Except that, like everything in life that seems to come for free, that affair at work cost me something too. When they offered me this job abroad for a year she decided to stay at home. The official reason was the children and that the move would be hard on them, but the truth was that maybe it suited both of us to be apart for a while. When I met Nicky it was long after I'd promised myself I'd never cheat on my wife again. But I did anyway, and it wasn't any great love story, nothing like that, just a chance to gain that much more life.

Parallel Universes

There's a theory that says there are billions of other universes, parallel to the one we live in, and that each of them is slightly different. There are the ones where you were never born, and the ones where you wouldn't want to be born. There are some parallel universes where I'm having sex with a horse, and ones where I won the lottery. There are universes where I'm lying on the bedroom floor, slowly bleeding to death, and universes where I've been elected president, by a landslide. But I don't care about any of those parallel universes now. The only ones that interest me are the ones where she isn't happily married, with a cute little boy, the ones where she's completely alone. There are plenty of universes like that, I'm sure. I'm trying to think about them now. Among all those universes, there are some

241

where we've never met. I don't care about those now. Among the ones that are left, there are some where she doesn't want me. She says no. In some of them she does it gently, and in others – in a way that hurts. I don't care about those now either. All that's left are the ones where she says yes, and I choose one of them, a little like you choose a piece of fruit at the greengrocer's. I choose the nicest one, the ripest one, the sweetest one. It's a universe where the weather is perfect, never too hot or too cold, and we live there in a little cottage in the woods. She works at the city library, a forty-minute drive from our home, and I work in the education department of the regional council, in the building that faces hers. Sometimes, from my office window, you can see her putting books back on the shelf. We always have our lunch together. And I love her and she loves me. And I love her and she loves me. And I love her and she loves me. I'd give anything to move to that kind of a universe. But meanwhile, until I find the way there, all I can do is think about it. I can picture myself living there in the middle of the woods. With her, in complete happiness. There's an infinite number of parallel universes in the world. In one of them I'm having sex with a horse, in another I've won the lottery. I don't want to think about those now, only about that one, the one with the cottage in the woods. There's a universe where I'm lying there with my wrists slashed, bleeding, on the bedroom floor. That's the universe that I'm doomed to live in until it's over. I don't want to think about it now. I just want to think about that other universe. A cottage in the woods, the sun setting, going to bed early. In bed, my right arm is unslashed, and dry. She's lying on it and we're hugging each other. She lies on it for so long that I can hardly feel it any more. But I don't move, I like it that way, with my arm under her warm body, and I keep liking it even when I can no longer feel my arm at all. I can sense her breathing on my face – rhythmic, regular, unending. My eyes begin to shut now. Not just in that universe, in bed, in the woods, but in the other universes too, the ones that I don't want to think about. I enjoy knowing there's one place, in the heart of the woods, where I'm falling asleep happy.

Upgrade

I talk too much. Sometimes when I'm talking and talking and talking that moment arrives – right there in the middle of the conversation – when I notice the person next to me has long stopped listening. He may keep up the nodding, but his eyes – they've completely clouded over. His mind has wandered, and he's thinking thoughts sweeter than the ones I share.

Of course, I could take issue with that assumption. I can pretty much argue anything. My wife says I'd get philosophical with a lamp post if I thought the thing had ears. I could've argued the point with the man sitting next to me – but there's no joy in it. He's already stopped listening. He's in another world. A better one (at least, in his opinion it is). And me? I keep on talking and talking and talking. It's like a car with the handbrake yanked, the wheels lock but it just goes on skidding down the road.

I want to stop talking. I do! But the words, the sentences, the ideas, there's a momentum to them, it's impossible to just stop them in their tracks, to seal up the lips and halt the words, right there, mid-sentence. There are people capable of doing it, I know.

Mainly women.

And when they go silent, it makes whoever's listening feel guilty. It spurs in the listener a yearning, a deep need to lean forward and hug them and say, 'I'm sorry.'

To say, 'I love you.'

I'd give up an eyeball to be able to do it, anything to have what it takes for that kind of on-a-sixpence stoppage. I'd make use of that gift all right. I'd just stop speaking next to the girls that really matter, and they'd just want to hug me, to squeeze me and say, 'I love you.' And even if they didn't actually do it, the fact that they'd wanted to would still be worth something. Worth a lot.

On this specific day, I can't stop talking next to a guy by the name of Michael. He's a graphic designer for a Hassidic newspaper in Brooklyn, flying from New York to Louisville, Kentucky, to sit in his uncle's sukkah. He's not especially close to this uncle, and not especially keen on Louisville. But his uncle sent him the ticket as a gift, and Michael is just mad about the frequent-flyer points. He's got a trip to Australia coming up, and with the points from the Louisville leg he'll be able to upgrade to business. On long flights, Michael tells me, the difference between business and economy, it's just day and night.

'What do you prefer,' I ask him, 'day or night?'

Because me, generally, I'm the night type, but the day also has some-something special about it, a radiance. At night it's quieter and colder, which is a significant consideration, at least for me, living as I do in tropical climes. But at night you're also liable to feel more alone if you don't have someone at your side, if you get my meaning . . . the one that I'm insinuating.

'I don't,' Michael says, his tone turned sharp.

'I'm not gay,' I tell him. Because I can see I've got him stressed. 'All this talk about loneliness and night-time sounds pretty much like textbook gay-talk, I know it. But I'm not. I've only kissed a guy on the mouth once, and that's in the whole thirty-plus years of my life, and even that was half by accident. This was back when I was in the army. There was a soldier by the name of Tzlil Drucker in my unit, and he'd brought some hash to the base, and suggested we smoke it. Tzlil asked if I'd ever smoked before, and I said, yes, I had. I hadn't intended to lie, it's just I've got a natural propensity for it. So pretty much when anyone asks me for anything and I'm under pressure I always answer, yes. Just – you know – to appease. It's a reflex that has the potential to complicate things for me, that's for sure. Picture this: a policeman walks into a room, sees me standing next to a corpse, and asks, 'Did you murder him?' That one's liable to end badly. The same policeman could also ask me something like, 'Are you innocent?' In that case, I'd come out of it all right. But really, between us, what're the chances that a policeman's going to ask it like that?

'So Tzlil and I smoked together, and it was a completely unique sensation. The drug, it just shut my mouth – plugged it up completely. I didn't have to speak in order to be. And during it, Tzlil told me that a year had gone by since he'd broken up with his girlfriend. That a year had gone by from the last time he'd kissed a woman. I remember he used that word, "woman". I told him that I'd never kissed a woman, or even a girl.

'"On the mouth", is what I meant. On the cheek I'd kissed loads. Aunties and the like. Anyway, Tzlil stared at me without saying a word, but I could see he was surprised. And then suddenly we were kissing. His tongue was rough and tangy, sort of like if you licked a rusty rail on the promenade. And I remember thinking back then, thinking that all the tongues and all the kisses that would ever be mine were going to feel just like that. And I also thought that never having kissed anyone until that day in my life, well, in essence, I hadn't missed a thing.

'Tzlil said, "I'm not a homo."

'And I laughed and said, "But your name is just fantastically gay."

'And that was that, basically.

'Eight years later, I bumped into him in some random hummus place and when I called him "Tzlil", he said he didn't go by that any more and that he'd gone down to the Ministry of the Interior and changed his name to Tzahi.

'I hope it wasn't on my account.'

Michael, who's sitting next to me, has long stopped listening. At the beginning, I thought he was all wound up because of the confusion about me coming on to him. Afterwards I began to suspect that he was actually gay, and that I'd insulted him with my story, that it was as if I were saying that kissing guys is gross. But when I look him in the eye, I find neither insult nor anxiety – just a bunch of frequent-flyer points accumulating towards an upgrade, towards more kindly flight attendants, towards higher quality coffee and enough leg room for a man to really stretch out.

When I see this, I feel guilty.

It isn't the first time I've seen that in the eyes of someone I'm talking to, and I don't mean the leg-room thing. I'm referring to the not-listening part – seeing that a person is thinking about something else completely. Always, I feel guilty. My wife says I shouldn't feel guilty, especially when my talking too much is so obviously a cry for help. She says the specific words coming out of my mouth don't matter at all, because what I'm really saying at any given moment is simply 'Help!' Think about it, she says. You're there screaming 'Help!'

and meanwhile they're thinking about something else. If anyone is supposed to feel guilty, it should be them, not you.

My wife's tongue is smooth and pleasant. Her tongue is the best place to be in the whole wide world. If it were only a little bit wider and a little bit longer, I'd move in for good. I'd roll myself up into that tongue – I'd be the crab to her California Roll, the eel to her Eel and Avocado. I tell you, thinking back to the tongue I started my kissing with and then looking at the tongue I ended up with, it wouldn't be unfair to say that I've really made something of this life of mine. That I've managed my own little version of an upgrade.

Truth be told, I've never once flown business class. But if the difference between that and economy is anything like the difference between my wife's tongue and the one in the mouth of Tzahi-Tzlil Drucker, I'd be ready to spend a week living in the coldest, dampest sukkah in the world with the stiffest, most boring uncle for the chance to get that kind of upgrade.

They announce overhead that we'll be landing in a little bit. I keep talking. Michael keeps not-listening. Planet Earth keeps spinning on its axis. Just another four days, my love. Another four days and I return to you. Another four days and, once again, I'll find it in my heart to shut up.

Guava

There was no sound from the engines of the plane. There were no sounds at all. Except perhaps the soft crying of the air stewardesses a few rows behind him. Through the elliptical window, Shkedi looked at the cloud hovering just below him. He could imagine the plane dropping through it like a stone, punching an enormous hole that would be sealed again quickly with the first breeze, leaving not so much as a scar. 'Just don't crash,' Shkedi said. 'Just don't crash.'

Forty seconds before Shkedi expired, an angel appeared, all dressed in white, and told him he'd been awarded a last wish. Shkedi tried to find out what 'awarded' implied. Was it an award like winning the lottery or was it something a bit more flattering: awarded in the sense of an achievement, in recognition of his good deeds? The angel shrugged. 'Dunno,' he said with pure angelic sincerity. 'They told me to come and fulfil, on the double. They didn't say why.' 'That's a shame,' Shkedi said. 'Because it's absolutely fascinating. Especially now, when I'm about to leave this world and everything, I'd really like to know if I'm leaving it as just another lucky guy or if I'm leaving it with a pat on the back.' 'Forty seconds and you kick off,' the angel droned. 'If you want to spend those forty seconds yapping, that's fine with me. No problem. Just consider that your window of opportunity is about to close.' Shkedi considered, and quickly made his wish. But not before taking the trouble to point out to the angel that he had a strange way of talking. For an angel, that is. The angel was hurt. 'What do you mean, for an angel? Have you ever heard an angel talk before, that you dump a thing like that on me?' 'Never,' Shkedi admitted. Suddenly, the angel looked much less angelic and much less pleasant, but that was nothing compared to what he looked like after he heard the wish.

'Peace on earth?' he screamed. 'Peace on earth? You're kidding me!'

And then Shkedi died.

Shkedi was dead and the angel was left behind. Left behind with the most bothersome and complicated wish he'd ever been asked to fulfil. Mostly, people ask for a new car for the wife, a flat for their daughter. Reasonable stuff. Specific stuff. But peace on earth is one hell of a job. First, the man hassles him with questions like he's Directory enquiries, then he has the audacity to put down the way he talks, and to top it off, he lands him with peace on earth. If Shkedi hadn't kicked the bucket, the angel would have stuck to him like herpes, and wouldn't have let go till he changed his wish. But the man's soul was in Seventh Heaven by now, and who knows how he'd ever find it.

The angel took a deep breath. 'Peace on earth, that's all,' he mumbled. 'Just peace on earth, that's all.'

And while all this was going on, Shkedi's soul completely forgot it had ever belonged to a person called Shkedi, and was reincarnated, pure and untainted, second-hand but good as new, as a piece of fruit. Yes, a piece of fruit. A guava.

The new soul had no thoughts. Guavas don't have thoughts. But it had feelings. It felt an overwhelming fear. It was afraid of falling off the tree.

Not that it had the words to describe this fear. But if it had, it would have been something like 'Oh my God, just don't crash!' And while it was hanging there, on the tree, petrified, peace began to reign on earth. People beat their swords into ploughshares and nuclear reactors soon began to be used for peaceful purposes. But none of this was of any comfort to the guava. Because the tree was tall and the ground seemed distant and painful. Just don't let me drop, the guava shuddered wordlessly, just don't crash.

Surprise Party

Three people are waiting at an intercom. A weird moment. More precisely, an awkward moment, uncomfortable.

'You're here for Avner's birthday too?' one of them, a man with a greying moustache, asks the man who rang the bell. The man who rang the bell nods. The third one, tall with a plaster on his nose, nods too. 'Really,' the moustache massages his neck nervously, 'you're friends of his?' They both nod. A female voice rings out from the intercom.

'Come on up, the twenty-first floor,' and then the buzz that opens the door. The lift buttons only go up to 21; our Avner lives in the penthouse.

On the way up, the moustache confesses that he doesn't really know Avner. The moustache is just the manager of the bank in Ramat Aviv where

Avner and Pnina Katzman have an account. He has never met them, didn't start at that branch till two months ago. Before that he managed a smaller branch in Ra'anana. That's why he was surprised when Pnina called to invite him to this party, but she insisted, said that Avner would be so happy.

Plaster-on-the-nose, it turns out, isn't really a close friend either. He's the husband's insurance broker, only met him a couple of times. And that was a while ago. For the last few years, they've been doing all their business by email.

The man who rang the bell, nice-looking, but with a monobrow, knows the Katzmans best. He's their dentist. He did four fillings for Pnina and made a crown for one of her molars. He also worked on Avner's teeth, one filling and a root canal, but he wouldn't really call himself a friend.

'It's strange that she invited us,' Moustache says.

'It's probably a big party,' Plaster decides.

'I wasn't planning to come,' Eyebrows admits, 'but Pnina is so sensitive.'

'Is she pretty?' Moustache asks. That's not a question a bank manager should ask, he knows. Eyebrows nods and shrugs at the same time as if to say, 'Yes, but what good will that do us?'

Pnina really is pretty. She's forty plus and looks it. No facelifts to keep the wrinkles away. If you could match a particular male sexual fantasy to every woman, Moustache thinks as he shakes her limp hand, then Pnina would be the perfect damsel-in-distress. There's a certain lack of confidence about her, a helplessness. Apart from the three of them, it turns out, no one has arrived yet. Just the catering staff, who are putting out more and more giant foil-covered bowls and trays jam-packed with canapés. No, Pnina assures them, they're not early. It's just the others who are late.

'It's my fault,' she explains. 'I decided on everything at the last minute. That's why I didn't invite any of you till today. I apologise.' Moustache says she has nothing to apologise for.

Eyebrows is already standing over one of the trays, getting to work on the bruschettas. So beautifully are they arranged that every one he takes is made conspicuous by its absence, like a pulled tooth.

He knows it's not very polite and he should wait for the rest of the guests, but he's dying of hunger. He operated on an old man's upper and lower gums today, a three-and-a-half-hour procedure, then he just changed his clothes and left for this party. He didn't even have time to go home first. He's hungry now, hungry and embarrassed. The bruschettas are good. He takes another one, his fifth, and walks off to stand at the side.

The living room of the flat is absolutely enormous, and there's also a glass door leading to the roof. Pnina tells them that she invited three hundred people, everyone she found listed in Avner's BlackBerry. Not all of them are coming, she knows, definitely not at such short notice, but it's going to be such fun.

The last time she organised a surprise party was ten years ago. They were living in India then because of Avner's business and one of the guests brought them a lion cub as a gift. In India, it seems, they're more flexible about laws for the preservation of wildlife, or maybe they just obey them less. That lion cub was the most adorable thing Pnina had ever seen in her life. In fact, that whole party was a tremendous success. Not that she's expecting anyone to bring them a lion today, but people are coming and they'll drink and laugh together, and it'll just be such fun.

'Letting ourselves go like that is just what we

all need, especially Avner, who's been working like a dog on the stock issue for the last few months,' Pnina says.

That story about India reminds Moustache of something – he brought a present too. He reaches into his pocket and takes out a long box wrapped in coloured paper imprinted with the bank's logo.

'It's just a little something,' he says in an apologetic tone, 'and it's not from me, it's from the entire branch.'

Anyway, it's hard to give a present after such an amazing story about a lion. Pnina says thank you and hugs Moustache – a rather surprising gesture considering they don't know each other, that, at least, is what Plaster thinks. Pnina insists that Moustache hold on to the present for the time being and give it to Avner personally.

She's sure, she says, that Avner will be so happy, he always loves presents.

That last remark makes Eyebrows feel uncomfortable for not bringing something. Plaster didn't bring a present either, but then again, he isn't eating anything, and Eyebrows has already finished off six bruschettas, two pieces of herring and some squid sushi, which, as the boy with the tray insisted on pointing out twice, isn't kosher. Eyebrows knows he shouldn't have come, but now all he can do is wait till Avner and the other guests turn up, and then, when everyone is busy partying, make his exit. But meanwhile, he's stuck here, he knows, totally stuck, and in the twenty minutes that have passed since he walked through the door, not one other guest has arrived.

'When did you say that Avner is supposed to get here?' Eyebrows asks, trying to be nonchalant. It doesn't work. Pnina gets upset.

'He should be here by now,' she says, 'but he doesn't know about the party, so maybe he'll be a little late.' She pours Eyebrows a glass of wine. He refuses politely, but she insists.

Plaster asks if there's any cognac. That makes Pnina very happy and she totters off to the drinks cabinet in her stiletto heels and takes out a bottle.

'The catering people probably have cognac,' she says, 'but not as good as this. This might not be enough for all the guests, but it is for our intimate little group, so let's make a toast.'

She pours cognac for Moustache and herself too, and they raise their glasses. Moustache, seeing that no one else is planning to say anything, quickly steps into the breach. He wishes all those present many parties and many surprises, nice ones, of course. And to Avner he wishes a speedy arrival, otherwise there won't be anything left for him to eat or drink. He and Pnina laugh.

Eyebrows feels as if that remark is somehow about him. True, he's eaten a lot since he came in, but he still thinks it's kind of nasty of Moustache to sell him out for a joke. And Pnina too – it's insulting, the way she's laughing at that tasteless bit of humour, exposing crowns that wouldn't be there if not for him. That's it, he decides, time to go. He'll do it politely so as not to hurt anyone's feelings, but with all due respect, he has a wife waiting at home, and all this place has to offer is a slightly tense atmosphere and non-kosher sushi.

Pnina's response to Eyebrows's stammered goodbye is extreme. 'You can't go,' she says, clutching his hand, 'this party is so important to Avner, and without you . . . as it is, almost no one else has come. But they'll be here,' she pulls herself together quickly, 'they probably just got held up on the road, there's heavy traffic at this hour, but if Avner arrives before them, he'll open the door and see only two people. Wonderful people, but only two. Not counting the catering crew, of course. That could be a disappointment. And the last thing anyone needs on his fiftieth birthday is a disappointment. It's a hard age as it is. And Avner hasn't had an easy time of it these last few months, so the last thing he needs when he comes in is to be welcomed by an empty living room.'

'Even three's not a lot,' Eyebrows maliciously states the obvious. The truth is, he adds, that if he were Pnina, he'd just cancel the whole thing and try to clear the place before Avner got home.

Pnina is quick to agree. She calls the catering manager over and tells him not to bring up any more food and to take his crew and wait downstairs in their van for the time being. When the rest of the guests arrive, she'll text them and they can come up again.

Till then, she explains to everyone without letting go of Eyebrows's hand, they'll all sit here in the living room and wait for Avner with a drink.

Maybe she should have planned something a little more intimate from the beginning. After all, fifty is not the age for wild dancing and loud music; fifty is more the age for stimulating conversation with close, insightful friends.

Eyebrows wanted to tell her that none of the people here are close to Avner, but he sees that she's already on the verge of tears and decides to keep quiet and let her drag him to the sofa. She sits him down and Plaster and Moustache join them.

Moustache is a world champion calmer-downer. He's already had more than a few conversations in his life with clients who lost all their money after the bottom fell out of one investment or another and he always knows how to act, especially with women. Now he bombards them with jokes, pours them all drinks, puts a comforting hand on Pnina's pale shoulder. If a stranger walked in, he'd probably think they were a couple.

Plaster seems pretty much at home too. What he has going for him is that he's in no great hurry to leave. He has a wife who always looks as if someone close to her has died, and an annoying two-year-old kid it's his turn to bath today.

Here, he can sit around, drink a bit, rub shoulders with someone who's had a bit more success in life than him, at least financially, and officially it could even be considered work.

Back home, whenever he gets there, he'll just

have to make a tired face and say they talked his head off all evening and all he could do was smile and take it because they're really good clients.

'That's how it is,' he'll tell his wife. 'To make a living, I have to listen to people's crap just like you have to . . .' and then he'll shut up as if he's forgotten, as if it just slipped his mind that she hasn't worked for more than two years and the entire financial burden falls on him alone.

She'll probably cry then, tell him that the post-natal depression isn't her fault, that it's a scientifically proven illness, that it's not just in her mind, it's chemical, like any other illness. She's dying to go back to work, if only she could, but she can't, she just can't . . . and he'll interrupt her stream of words and apologise, say he didn't mean anything, that the words just slipped out of his mouth. And she'll believe him, or not. With all that wasteland between them, what does it really matter.

Moustache seems to pick up on everything that's going through Plaster's mind and pours him a little more cognac.

That Moustache is something, Plaster thinks, a special guy. Eyebrows, on the other hand, is kind of neurotic and makes him nervous. When they first got here, he kept eating the whole time and now he just looks at his watch and scratches himself. Before, when Pnina tried to persuade him to stay, he almost wanted to break into the conversation and tell her to leave him alone, to just let him go. No one needs him here. You might think he's Avner's childhood friend or something when he's just some guy who drilled his teeth.

And anyway, when he thinks about it, it's a little strange that they're the only ones who came. What does that say about Avner's really close friends? That they're so egotistical? That he's offended them? Or maybe he just doesn't have any?

The intercom buzzes and Pnina runs to answer it. Moustache winks at Eyebrows and Plaster and pours another round of cognac. 'Don't worry,' he says to Eyebrows, as if he's another customer of the bank who's fallen on bad times, 'it'll be fine.'

It's just the catering manager on the intercom. Their van is blocking someone. He asks if he can park in the building car park. Before Pnina can answer, the phone rings. She hurries over to pick up the receiver. Silence on the other end.

'Avner,' she says, 'where are you? Is everything

OK?' She knows it's Avner because his number is on the display. But there's no answer at the other end, just the drone of a dead line.

Panina starts to cry, but it's a weird kind of crying. Her eyes are wet and her whole body trembles, but she doesn't make a sound, like a mobile phone on vibrate. Moustache goes over and takes the cognac glass out of her hand a second before it would have fallen and shattered.

'He's not OK,' Pnina says, throwing her arms around Moustache, 'something isn't right with him. I knew it, this whole time I knew it. That's why I decided to have the party, to cheer him up.'

Moustache takes her to the sofa and sits her down next to Eyebrows.

Eyebrows is getting stressed. When Pnina came back from answering the phone, he planned to tell her that he had to go. His wife is waiting for him or something, but now he knows he can't. Pnina's sitting so close to him now that he can hear her irregular breathing. And her face is totally pale. It looks like she's going to faint.

Plaster brings a glass of water and Moustache puts it to her lips. She drinks a little and starts to calm down.

That was a scary moment, Eyebrows thinks.

I wonder what he said to her on the phone, Plaster thinks.

Even when she's weak, Moustache thinks, even when she's on the verge of collapse, she's all woman. Deep in his trousers, he feels the beginning of an erection and hopes no one else notices.

The intercom buzzes. It's the catering manager again; he's waiting for an answer about parking in the building car park. Traffic's crazy now and finding a spot on the street for a large van is just impossible. Plaster, who answered the buzz, repeats the question out loud.

Moustache gives him a tell-him-it's-OK nod. But the semi-conscious Pnina mumbles that he shouldn't use the tenants' car park. There's a neighbour on the seventeenth floor who causes problems. Just last week, an acquaintance who dropped in to see her for an hour, even less, got towed away.

Eyebrows volunteers to go downstairs and tell the caterers they can't use the building car park. From there, he thinks, the way home will be shorter.

Moustache says he should stay, Pnina isn't doing

well and it would be better to have a doctor around. 'I'm a doctor of dentistry,' Eyebrows says.

'You're a doctor of dentistry, I know,' Mustache counters.

Pnina says that they have to go to Avner's office right now. It's not like him to call and then hang up like that. Anyway, something's been wrong with him lately. He's always taking pills. He told Pnina they were for headaches, but Pnina knows headache pills, and what Avner's taking isn't paracetamol or ibruprofen, it's this black, elliptical pill that isn't like any other pill she's ever seen before. And at night he has nightmares, she knows, because she's heard him calling out in his sleep.

'Talk to Cohavi,' he shouts, 'talk to Cohavi.' When she asked him about it, he said everything was fine and he doesn't know anyone called Cohavi.

But she knows that he does. Igal Cohavi. His phone number is in Avner's BlackBerry. And of all the numbers listed there, his was the only one she didn't call. She thought he might put a damper on the atmosphere.

'I don't know what's going to happen,' Pnina says, 'I'm scared.'

269

Moustache nods and says that all four of them should go to Avner's office to see if he's OK.

Eyebrows says that they're all getting a bit carried away here and the first thing Pnina should do is call him again. Their phone conversation got cut off; things like that happen all the time. Something might be wrong with Avner, but something might be wrong with the phone company too, and they should check it out before they schlep all the way to Herzliya.

With shaking hands, Pnina punches in Avner's office number. She puts the phone on speaker. Plaster thinks that's strange. What if Avner picks up and tells her something intimate or insulting; that could be awkward.

But there's no answer at the other end. Eyebrows says she should try Avner's mobile, so Pnina tries. A recorded announcement tells her she's reached Avner Katzman and anyone who needs him urgently should call his secretary or text him because he doesn't listen to messages.

Moustache doesn't know Avner, but just from his diction he can tell he wouldn't like him. There's something haughty about his voice, the voice of someone who thinks everything is coming to him, a kind of *noblesse oblige* without the *oblige*.

A lot of the clientele at Moustache's Ra'anana branch were like that, the kind of people who were offended every time the bank charged them a fee. The way they saw it, just agreeing to open an account in Moustache's branch was already a huge gift they'd given to the bank, and how rude, not to mention ungrateful, of the bank to still charge them for a new chequebook or expect them to pay interest on overdrawn funds after they'd made such a lovely gesture.

Eyebrows asks Pnina to text Avner, but Moustache interrupts him, saying they have no more time to waste and they should all drive to his office now. Plaster agrees quickly; this whole business seems like an adventure to him.

The truth is that he's not worried about Avner killing himself because his life insurance policy doesn't cover suicide, but now, even if Plaster doesn't get home till four in the morning, he can tell his wife it had to do with work.

They all go in Moustache's car, a new Honda Civic. In the lift, Eyebrows still tries to convince them to split up – he and Plaster would take his car – but Moustache firmly vetoes the idea.

Plaster and Eyebrows sit in the back with their

seat belts buckled like two kids on a Saturday family outing. The only thing missing is for Eyebrows to complain to Moustache, 'Daddy, Plaster's teasing me,' or to ask him to stop at a petrol station because he has to do a wee.

Eyebrows is capable of stuff like that, he's a real baby. If there was a war on now, Moustache thinks, and lots of people say there is, Eyebrows is the last person he'd want watching his back. Avner is a pain in the arse, that much is clear already, but still, your patient disappears, his wife is an emotional wreck and all you can think about is bruschettas and getting home early?

Eyebrows is texting in the back, probably to his wife, probably something sarcastic. Plaster is trying to sneak a look at the message, but the angle is wrong. A minute later, when Eyebrows receives an answer, he can read it, and it says, 'I'm waiting for you in bed wearing just my socks.'

That makes Plaster jealous. He has never received a sexy text message. The last time his wife wanted to say anything sexy to him was before texting was invented and he doesn't let all those women he fucks on the side text him or leave voicemail. He once read in a newspaper that even if you delete messages, the mobile phone company still has copies and they can blackmail you or just screw up your life.

There's heavy traffic all the way to Herzliya. Everyone who works in Tel Aviv is on his way home now. Traffic in the other direction is actually light.

Eyebrows can picture Avner driving home now after a completely ordinary day's work. In that phone conversation, he'd probably wanted to tell Pnina that he loved her, that he's sorry he's been a little stressed out these last few days, and also for lying about the black pills. They're for haemorrhoids, and he was too embarrassed to tell her, so he tried to sell her a story about headaches.

And when he gets home he'll see some pissed-off people in a caterer's van fighting over a parking space with one of the neighbours and he'll think some Buddhist thought like how many of our fights in life are about trivialities, then he'll skip over to the lift and when he reaches his floor and opens the door, he'll find a completely empty flat and a half-empty bottle of cognac.

Pnina won't be there and that'll really hurt. After all, today's his birthday. He doesn't need presents or parties from her, they're past the age for that kind of crap, but is it too much to ask your life partner to be with you, just be with you on your bloody birthday? And, Eyebrows thinks, at the very same time, Pnina is in a traffic jam on the way to Herzliya. What a joke.

But Avner isn't driving to his flat in Ramat Aviv now. And he isn't in his office in Herzliya either.

When the four of them finally get there, there's no one in the office, but the security guard at the entrance says he saw Avner leave less than an hour ago. He says Avner had a gun. He knows that because Avner asked him to help cock it. Not that Avner didn't know how to do that, he did, but something was stuck and he wanted the security guard to help him get it unstuck.

Except that the security guard wasn't exactly the right person for the job; he was just an old Kazakhi who had grown vegetables in some remote village his whole life, not Rambo. When he came to Israel he asked to work as a farmer, but the people in the agency said no, only Thais and Arabs work in farming today and what he can do from now till he dies is retire or be a security guard.

He tells Moustache that when he couldn't help with the gun, Avner got angry with him and even started swearing.

'It's not nice,' the security guard says. 'It's not nice to swear at a man my age. And for what? I did something wrong?'

Moustache nods. He knows that if he wants to, he can calm down the security guard too, but he doesn't have the energy any more. And that talk about the gun bothers him. All the way here he was thinking Pnina might be exaggerating with all that worrying of hers, but now he sees she's really right.

'If he asked me about agriculture, I could help him with everything,' the guard says to Plaster, 'I like to help. But about guns, I don't know. So that is a reason to swear?'

On the way back to the car, Pnina is crying. Eyebrows says that this whole business is out of their hands now, they have to call the police.

Plaster butts in, claiming that the police won't do a thing. If you don't have connections it takes at least a day before they start moving their arses. Not that Plaster has a better plan than going to the police, but Eyebrows has been getting on his nerves for a while now and the last thing he wants is to agree with him about anything.

Moustache strokes Pnina's hair. He doesn't have a plan either; he can't think at all while she's crying. Her tears flood his brain, drowning all thoughts before they can be completed. And the fact that Plaster and Eyebrows are arguing next to him – that doesn't exactly help his concentration either.

'You two take a taxi. You can't help here any more,' he tells them.

'What about you and Pnina?' Plaster asks. He really doesn't want to go, or pay for a cab, or drive all the way to Ramat Aviv with Eyebrows.

Moustache shrugs. He has no answer to that.

'He's right,' Eyebrows says, knowing that this is his chance to take off, and besides, Moustache is really right, the fact that there are four of them doesn't help anything. Moustache can drive to the police station with Pnina alone, he doesn't need them to come along and hold his hand.

Plaster isn't happy with the whole idea; now that there's a gun and some action, going home would be a real downer. If he stays he can change something, maybe save that Avner, and even if he doesn't and he just finds his body with Moustache and

Pnina, that would be an experience he'd probably remember for the rest of his life. Maybe not the greatest experience, but still, an experience.

He hasn't had too many of those these last few years. There was the blast wave of that missile landing near their guest house in the north, shattering the window, and a basketball game he went to once with a friend and the TV cameras caught him yawning. Maybe also when his son was born. Even though he wasn't really there for it. His wife made him leave the delivery room a few minutes before because she was angry at him for answering a call from someone at work.

In short, Plaster isn't keen on leaving, but he knows that if Moustache and Eyebrows are against him, he can't insist on staying without seeming like an arsehole. The only way to save the situation now is to come up with an idea. A killer idea that'll lead to a plan and put him right in the centre of things as the originator, someone useful, someone worth having around.

'We have to talk to Igal Cohavi,' he says, partly to Moustache, partly to Pnina, who's stopped crying now and is just panting, 'Pnina said she has his number from Avner's BlackBerry. And if he had a dream about him that made him cry out, Avner must really have him on his mind. Who knows, that whole story with the gun makes it look like he's going to commit suicide, but what if he's planning to kill that Cohavi instead? We should call and warn him, find out.'

As soon as Plaster says 'commit suicide', Pnina starts crying again, and when he says 'kill', she faints dead away.

Luckily, Moustache manages to catch her a second before her face hits the pavement.

Plaster runs over to Moustache to help, but the look on Moustache's face makes it clear that that's not a good idea.

Eyebrows says it's nothing, just the pressure. Someone should get her a glass of water, sit her down on a bench and she'll be back to normal in no time.

'Get out of here, both of you,' Moustache yells, 'get out of here, now.'

Later, in the taxi, Plaster will tell Eyebrows that Moustache went too far; who is he to talk to them like that? These days, if an officer talks to his soldiers like that, he gets a formal complaint lodged against him, so who the hell is Moustache to yell that way at two people he barely knows and who are only trying to help?

That's what he'll say later, in the taxi. But now, outside the office building in Herzliya Pituach, Plaster doesn't say anything, and he and Eyebrows walk away, leaving Moustache and Pnina alone.

Moustache carries her to the car and puts her in the passenger seat gently, as if she were a fragile object. Pnina comes to even before they reach the car and mumbles something, her eyes half closed, but only after he puts her down does he start to listen.

'I'm thirsty,' she says.

'I know,' Moustache says, 'I don't have any water in the car, I'm sorry. We can drive somewhere to buy a bottle. On the way here, really nearby, I saw a branch of Aroma.'

'Do you think he's dead already?' she asks.

'Who?' Moustache asks.

He knows who she means but pretends not to – that's a trick meant to make her fear seem unfounded. She looks at him but doesn't say 'Avner' like he thought she would. All she does is look at him.

'I'm sure he's fine,' Moustache says. His voice

sounds convincing. It's the voice that got him the Ra'anana branch and now the one in Ramat Aviv.

'I'm scared,' Pnina says, just as he'd imagined her saying it the first time he saw her that evening. She's so beautiful when she says it.

Moustache leans forward and kisses her dry lips. Her lips move away from his. He doesn't see anything, doesn't even notice her hand move, but his cheek feels the slap.

When Eyebrows gets home, his wife is already asleep. He doesn't feel the slightest bit tired. His body is exploding with adrenalin. Eyebrows's mind knows that all the fainting and waiting and weird arguments tonight were all about nothing, but his body is stupid enough to take it seriously. Instead of getting into bed he sits down in front of the computer and checks his emails.

The only message he has is from some idiot who went to primary school with him and found his email address through an Internet site.

That's what's so frustrating about all that technology, Eyebrows thinks. The ones who invented the Internet were geniuses and probably believed they were advancing humanity, but in the end, instead of people using all that ingenuity to do research and gain knowledge, they use it to harass some poor guy who sat next to them in the fourth year.

What exactly is he supposed to write back to that Yiftach Rozales? You remember how we drew a line right down the middle of the desk? How you used to elbow me in the ribs when I crossed it?

Eyebrows tries to imagine what Yiftach Rozales's life is like if all he has to do in his free time is search for some boy he never really liked who was in his class thirty years ago.

After a few minutes of feeling superior to Rozales, Eyebrows starts thinking about himself. And exactly what is he doing with his life? Bending over smelly mouths, drilling and filling cavities in rotten teeth.

'A highly respected profession,' that's what his mother always says when she talks about dentistry.

What is there to respect? What actually is the difference between being a dentist and being a plumber? They both work in smelly holes, drilling and filling openings to make a living. Both earn decent money. And it's highly probable that neither one really enjoys his profession.

Except that Eyebrows's work is 'highly respected', and to gain that respect, Eyebrows had to leave the country for five years to study in Romania while the plumber probably had to invest a little less time.

Today was really the worst, operating on the gums of that old man who never stopped wailing and bleeding, practically choking on the suction. And Eyebrows, who kept trying to calm him down, couldn't stop thinking that it was all for nothing. That it would take that old man at least a year of suffering to get used to the implants and probably two days before or after that he'll die of a heart attack or cancer or a stroke or whatever it is people his age die of.

There should be an age limit for patients, he thinks as he takes off his shoes. You just have to say to them, 'You've lived long enough. From now on, think of what's left as a bonus, a gift without an exchange note. It hurts? Stay in bed. It still hurts? Wait: either you'll die or it'll pass.'

That age, Eyebrows thinks to himself as he brushes his teeth, is on its way to me, galloping like a wild horse spraying foam from its nostrils. Soon it'll be me lying in that bed not getting up. And something about that thought comforts him.

The last time, the only other time that Pnina ever slapped someone, it was Avner. That was seventeen years ago. He wasn't rich yet, or bitter or balding, but he already exuded that confidence that everything was his. It was their first date and they went to a restaurant.

Avner was nasty to the waiter and made him take back his food, which wasn't fantastic, but decent enough. She couldn't work out what she was doing at the same table with this arrogant man.

Her flatmate had set them up. She'd told Pnina that Avner was brilliant and she'd told Avner that Pnina was charming, which was actually her way of saying that she was pretty without feeling like a chauvinist.

Avner spent the whole evening talking to her about stocks and derivatives and institutional investors and didn't let her get a word in edgeways. After dinner he drove her to her flat in his battered white Autobianchi. He stopped in front of her building, turned off the engine and suggested going up with her.

She said she didn't think that was a good idea. He reminded her that he knew her flatmate and that he just wanted to go upstairs for a minute to say hello to her. Hello and thanks for introducing them.

Pnina smiled politely and said that her flatmate would be back late because she was working the night shift. She promised to give her his regards and pass on his thanks and already had the door open to get out, but Avner closed it and kissed her.

There was no hesitation, no wondering how she felt there on the other side of the kiss. It was just a kiss on the mouth, but it felt like rape.

Pnina slapped him and got out of the car. Avner didn't try to follow or call her. From the flat balcony, she could see his Autobianchi standing there, not moving. For maybe an hour. It was still there when Pnina went to sleep.

In the morning, a delivery man woke her with a huge and slightly tasteless bouquet of flowers. There was only one word written on the card. Sorry.

'I'm sorry,' Moustache says, 'I didn't mean it.'

And Pnina could have been tough on him, could have asked him what exactly did he mean, kissing her? Taking advantage of her weakness? Driving all the way to Herzliya with her in a car that smelled of coconut air-freshener mixed with sweat? But she doesn't say anything, she doesn't have the strength. She just wants Moustache to take her home.

'Maybe we should go to the police,' Moustache says, 'just to be on the safe side.'

But Pnina says no. Avner will come home in the end, she just knows it, he's not the kind to commit suicide or shoot someone. After Plaster said that, it scared her at first, but now when she tries to picture Avner sticking the gun in his mouth or pressing it against his temple – it's just not him. When she looks at her hands she can see they are shaking, but her mind has already decided that Avner is all right.

Moustache doesn't argue, he just drives Pnina home.

The catering van is parked outside with two wheels on the pavement, still blocking the street. Poor guys, they've been waiting there the whole time. Moustache says he'll get out and talk to them. He wants to help her with something, to make up for what happened. But she doesn't let him. Not to punish him, she just doesn't have the energy.

After Pnina gets out of the car, he calls after her. The rage she felt earlier is gone now. She's not angry at him any more, really. He actually seems like a nice person. And that kiss – maybe his timing was a little off, but she sensed how much he wanted her from the moment he arrived, and for most of the evening it made her feel good.

Moustache gives her the gift for Avner and his business card, explaining that his mobile number is on the card too and she can call him no matter how late. She nods.

She won't call him, not today.

Plaster finds a parking spot right outside his building. But instead of going up to the second floor, putting his key in the lock, taking off his clothes in the dark hallway and creeping quietly to his side of the bed, he starts to walk. At first, he has no idea where he's headed: Shtand Street, King Solomon, King George, then Dizengoff Street. Only on Dizengoff does he realise that he wants to go to the sea.

He keeps walking till he reaches the promenade, and from there he goes down to the beach. He takes off his shoes and socks and just stands there, scooping up the sand with his toes. Behind him he can hear the noise of traffic and trance music probably coming from an all-night off-licence. In front of him, he hears the sound of the waves crashing against the breakwater not far from there.

'Excuse me,' a young guy with an army buzzcut says, appearing out of nowhere, 'you live here?'

Plaster nods.

'Great,' Buzzcut says, 'so maybe you know where to go for some fun?'

Plaster can ask him what kind of fun he means: alcohol? girls? a mysterious blast of warmth flooding your chest? What's the point, he doesn't know where to find any of those things, so he just shakes his head.

But Buzzcut persists. 'You said you live here, right?'

Plaster doesn't answer, just looks to the distant point where the black of the sea meets the black of the sky.

I wonder what happened to that Avner, he thinks. I hope that in the end, it all worked out.

What Animal Are You?

The sentences I'm writing now are for the benefit of the German Public Television viewers. A reporter who came to my home today asked me to write something on the computer because it always makes for great visuals: an author writing. It's a cliché, she realises that, but clichés are nothing but an unsexy version of the truth, and her role, as a reporter, is to turn that truth into something sexy, to break the cliché with lighting and unusual angles. And the light in my house falls perfectly, without her having to turn on even a single spot, so all that's left is for me to write.

At first, I just made believe I was writing, but she said it wouldn't work. People would be able to tell right away that I was just pretending. 'Really write something,' she demanded, and then, to be clear: 'A story, not just a load of words. Write naturally, the way you always do.' I told her it wasn't natural for me to be writing while I was having my picture taken for German Public Television, but she insisted. 'So use it,' she said. 'Write a story about just that – about how unnatural it seems and how the unnaturalness suddenly produces something real, filled with passion. Something that permeates you, from your brain to your loins. Or the other way round. I don't know how it works with you, what part of your body gets the creative juices flowing. Each person is different.' She told me how she'd once interviewed a Belgian author who, every time he wrote, had an erection. Something about the writing 'stiffened his organ' – that's the expression she used. It was probably a literal translation from German and it sounded very strange in English.

'Write,' she insisted again. 'Great. I love your terrible posture when you write, the cramped neck. It's just wonderful. Keep writing. Excellent. That's it. Naturally. Don't mind me. Forget I'm here.'

So I go on writing, not minding her, forgetting she's there, and I'm natural. As natural as I can be. I have a score to settle with the viewers of German Public Television but this isn't the time to settle it. This is the time to write. To write things that will appeal, because when you write crap, she's already reminded me, it comes out terrible on camera.

My son returns from nursery. He runs up to me and hugs me. Whenever there's a television crew in the house, he hugs me. When he was younger, the reporters had to ask him to do it, but by now, he's a pro: runs up to me, doesn't look at the camera, gives me a hug, and says: 'I love you, Daddy.' He isn't four yet, but he already understands how things work, this adorable son of mine.

My wife isn't as good, the German Public Television reporter says. She doesn't flow. Keeps fiddling with her hair, stealing glances at the camera. But that isn't really a problem. You can always edit her out later. That's what's so nice about television. In real life it isn't like that. In real life you can't edit her out, undo her. Only God can do that, or a bus, if it runs her over. Or a terrible disease. Our upstairs neighbour is a widower. An incurable disease took his wife from him. Not cancer, something else. Something that starts in the guts and ends badly. For six months she was shitting blood. At least that's what he told me. Six months before God Almighty edited her out. Ever since she died, all kinds of women keep visiting our building, wearing high heels and cheap perfume. They arrive at unlikely hours, sometimes as early as noon. He's retired, our upstairs neighbour, and his time is his own. And those women, according to my wife at least, they're whores. When she says 'whores' it comes out naturally, like she was saying 'turnip'. But when she's being filmed, it doesn't. Nobody's perfect.

My son loves the whores who visit our upstairs neighbour. 'What animal are you?' he asks them when he bumps into them on the stairs. 'Today I'm a mouse, a quick and slippery mouse.' And they get it right away, and throw out the name of an animal: an elephant, a bear, a butterfly. Each whore and her animal. It's strange, because with other people, when he asks them about the animals, they just don't catch on. But the whores go along with it.

Which gets me thinking that the next time a television crew arrives I'll use one of them instead of my wife, and that way it'll be more natural. They look great. Cheap, but great. And my son gets along better with them too. When he asks my wife what animal she is, she always insists: 'I'm not an animal, sweetie, I'm a person. I'm your mummy.' And then he always starts to cry.

Why can't she just go with the flow, my wife? Why is it so easy for her to call women with cheap perfume 'whores' but when it comes to telling a little boy 'I'm a giraffe' it's more than she can handle? It really gets on my nerves. Makes me want to hit someone. Not her. Her I love. But someone. To take out my frustrations on someone who has it coming. Right-wingers can take it out on Arabs. Racists on blacks. But those of us who belong to the liberal left are trapped. We've boxed ourselves in. We have nobody to take it out on. 'Don't call them whores,' I go on at my wife. 'You don't know for a fact that they're whores, do you? You've never seen anyone pay them or anything, so don't call them that, OK? How would you feel if someone called you a whore?'

'Great,' the German reporter says. 'I love it. The crease in your forehead. The frenzied keystrokes. Now all we need are an intercut with translations of your books in different languages, so our viewers can tell how successful you are – and that hug from your son one more time. The first time he ran up to you so quickly that Jörg, our cameraman, didn't have a chance to change the focus.' My wife wants to know if the German reporter needs her to hug me again too, and in my heart I pray she'll say yes. I'd really love my wife to hug me again, her smooth arms tightening around me, as if there's nothing else in the world but us. 'No need,' the German says in an icy voice. 'We've got that already.' 'What animal are you?' my son asks the German, and I quickly translate into English. 'I'm not an animal,' she laughs, running her long fingernails through his hair. 'I'm a monster. A monster that came from across the ocean to eat pretty little children like you.' 'She says she's a songbird,' I translate to my son with impeccable naturalness. 'She says she's a red-feathered songbird, who flew here from a faraway land.'

www.vintage-books.co.uk